THE
BODY
HARVEST

a novel by
Michael J. Seidlinger

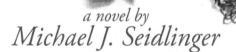

CLASH
HORROR

Troy, NY
CLASH Books
clashbooks.com

HORROR

 @clashbooks  @clashbooks clashbooks

Email: clashmediabooks@gmail.com

"Do not, under any circumstance, read when you're alone. One of the most disturbing novels I've read in years."

—Danielle Trussoni, New York Times Book Review

"This book makes *Cabin at the End of the World* by Paul Tremblay look like a cakewalk. This is THE MOST intense psychological horror you have ever read. Seriously. It makes *Out* by Natsuo Kirino look tame."

—Library Journal (Starred Review)

"Guaranteed to give you goosebumps and double (or triple) check the locks on your doors."

—Buzzfeed

"*Anybody Home?* is an uncomfortable triumph. It's a book that will satisfy fans of Seidlinger's chameleonic voice, and will make new fans of those who haven't read his work yet."

—Gabino Iglesias, Locus Magazine

"Harrowing and tremendously upsetting, *Anybody Home?* flips the home invasion genre on its head for a new generation of readers. I felt like I was reading something I shouldn't have been reading. You'll be checking your locks regularly after reading this nasty little morsel."

—Eric LaRocca, author of *Things Have Gotten Worse Since We Last Spoke* & *Everything the Darkness Eats*

"A bone-chilling, immersive horror novel that explores fear, obsession, voyeurism, and senseless violence. Seidlinger takes an ax to the illusion of suburban safety. Unsettling, unflinching, and unforgettable. *Anybody Home?* is one of the most terrifying books I've ever read."

—Rachel Harrison, author of *Cackle* and *Such Sharp Teeth*

"Michael J. Seidlinger is a true innovator. The narrative shards of *Anybody Home?* cascade over the reader in a collage of troubling, sometimes half-seen images, and the wicked, insinuating, deeply unsettling voice weaves through the back of your mind and crouches in your dreams. A chilling and unforgettable book."

—Dan Chaon, author of *Sleepwalk*

"Damn, this book is effed up."

—CrimeReads

"An ice cold, deadpan zeitgeist nightmare, Michael J. Seidlinger knows, and shows, that even in a lockdown moment, home is the most dangerous place of all. Watch out. Too late. They're watching you."

—Kathe Koja, author of *Dark Factory*

"*Anybody Home?* is an immersive novel that deconstructs home invasions for sport, resulting in addictive commentary on the horror genre itself."

—Foreword Reviews (starred review)

"*Anybody Home?* is *Natural Born Killers* for a generation that grew up on *Funny Games, The Purge,* and Twitter. An incisive commentary on how, in our culture, everything eventually gets mediatized—and a how-to guide to some of the darkest corners of that process, one that implicates you even as you read it."

—Brian Evenson, author of *Song for the Unraveling of the World*

"With this sinister and alluring story of home invasions, Michael Seidlinger has invented a new type of horror novel, one that simultaneously chronicles the characters' transgressions and the audience's reactions. It's a searing commentary on voyeurism and mass media, as well as a riff on Michael Haneke's *Funny Games* that outdoes the original. Read it with the doors locked."

—Jeff Jackson, author of *Destroy All Monsters*

"Perhaps the most immersive home invasion story you will ever read. It's like having a madman confess his sins in your ear. Absolutely chilling."

—Ronald Malfi, author of *Come with Me*

"Seidlinger pulls no punches in delivering gut-wrenching horror as he drives the novel to its bloody conclusion. Fans of Jack Ketchum and Samantha Kolesnik will want to check this out."

—Publishers Weekly

"This addictive deconstruction of the home invasion is so thorough and chilling, Seidlinger may as well have slammed the door on the entire genre. But beyond the torture and violation, *Anybody Home?* is a nuanced study of the creative process, exploring what it takes to create art that truly resonates."

—B.R. Yeager, author of *Negative Space*

"*Anybody Home?* is a literal and metaphorical dissection of the nuclear family, executed with panache and filled with cutting insights. Seidlinger knows precisely how to make the reader complicit. These pages will bloody your hands, and it'll be a long time before the stains wash clean."

—Brian Asman, author of *Man, Fuck This House*

"Michael J. Seidlinger's *Anybody Home?* isn't just a deliriously terrifying novel, it's also a ransom note from our fame-obsessed id. It's an instruction manual from evil itself, and it's a mirror trick that puts you behind the eyes of a monster, only to realize the prey being stalked… is also you."

—Nat Cassidy, author of *Mary: An Awakening of Terror*

"In *Anybody Home?*, Michael J. Seidlinger so masterfully crafts an atmosphere of pure terror that it had me checking to make sure my front door was locked, for fear of home invaders—or maybe Seidlinger himself."

—Rob Hart, author of *The Paradox Hotel*

"Michael J. Seidlinger's *Anybody Home?* is unflinching in its execution, offering a cold and quiet intensity matched only by its scathing indictment of entertainers and the entertained. It might be the scariest book I've read in a decade."

—Todd Keisling, Bram Stoker Award-nominated author of *Devil's Creek* and *Scanlines*

"In Michael J. Seidlinger's *Anybody Home?* your security alarm and cameras are positioned to betray you. Our invaders and our victims have been chosen carefully to perform in this meticulous, intoxicating, and brutal tale of home invasion."

—Cynthia Pelayo, three-time Bram Stoker Award® nominated author of *Children of Chicago*

"I wanted to rub the human race in its own vomit, and force it to look in the mirror."

—J.G. Ballard

"It was better to be alone than to be stuck with people who were supposed to love you, yet couldn't."

— Ottessa Moshfegh

THE

BODY HARVEST

M. J. Seidlinger

Part One

THE
SOURCE

CHAPTER

I

You never know until it's too late what might be incubating in your body, metastasizing to become the next name you can't forget. He coughs in her face. She breathes in, mouth wide, anticipating a few droplets to make it up the bridge of her nose, into the inner sanctum of her body, a wanton new host to incubate. She keeps her eyes closed, but it's clear that she can barely tolerate the anticipation. Their faces inches from each other, he watches as his own saliva lands on her face, a noticeable streak of phlegm on her right cheek. It's how they don't hold each other close, how he clears his throat and coughs a second time that makes it quite clear that what's happening here is an entirely different sort of transaction. That's him, Will, who has started to come down with something. She opens her eyes after the second cough, can sense the fluids on her face, yet waits a few moments before wiping them on her sleeve. That's her, Olivia, who would be, by any sense of the term, healthy, which is enough to make her come out of her own skin.

"Think it's enough?" she asks.

That razor-sharp scraping sound of the folds of his throat rubbing together, he offers her a third, "Just in case."

She grins, says nothing more. Eyes once again closed, it's a delicate sort of intimacy shared. Will once again coughs in her face, and then he spits into his palm, the bright yellow phlegm produced is a telltale sign of something on the horizon.

"Took two days," he says, as if reading her mind.

"I see," she says, looking at the drying streak on the sleeve of her hoodie. "I'm forgetting the last time I crashed."

That gets his attention, balling his fist, the fluids pressed shut against the folds of his palm. "How does it feel?"

"I feel vulnerable," she confesses. "I don't know what to do with myself. It's like everything is…"

Will reaches for the answer like it's the only thing he's ever known. "Like it's too vivid. Like you're watching TV with the contrast way up."

"Way *way* up," she says, nodding. Olivia digs her nails into her wrist, the anxiety palpable enough to keep her from sitting still. "You said it took two days?"

Their bodies almost touching, depending on the angle of the capture, they could be mistaken for something else. Look closely and you'll see that they avoid even the accidental touch. His hands rest close to his chest, her arms wrap around her own body. They can feel the heat emanating from each other, yet maybe that's not actually true. Olivia cocks her head to the side, "Fever?"

He's quick with the draw, "Checked a half hour ago. 100.1F."

She bites her lower lip, "Hmm. Seems off."

That strikes a nerve, causing him to look away. "It's definitely something. I assure you."

"I don't doubt it," she says, keen to his vulnerability. "But after two days… this is just another Chris. Maybe a Jeff."

Will exhales, causing him to gag slightly. He lets whatever made the trek up his throat roll off his tongue and drip into his lap. More yellow phlegm, no signs of a reddish speckle. The way he won't come out and say it proves it all. Whatever he has, it's nothing more potent than when they dealt with Chris. Ah, Chris. That was at least two weeks ago. Perhaps in line with when they first met. Mild fever, extensive cough, some malaise, nothing spectacular. He made it work though, really laid into it, hoping that it might worsen before the symptoms let up and his body fought Chris off, a thing of the past.

"It can be enough," he says.

"I hope it can be enough."

Enough. That's always changing. Chris offered him four days, maybe five. Chris didn't even bother with Olivia. There have been plenty of others, all of them conquered, but there's added pressure between them because since they've met, there hasn't been a name that stuck. Olivia remembers being bedridden for almost a month. Will thought Lars was going to finally end his life. But it didn't. Neither succumbed and instead, as they like to call it, they conquered both, and then they went searching and found each other.

"I do feel a little different." A statement that's designed to make her feel better. The reality is, this doesn't feel like anything new. Will's going to kick this by the end of the weekend. He'll cough, feel a little lightheaded, ooze phlegm and bile, but there'll be a swift move for recovery. "I think I'm going to lay down."

There he goes, standing up and making a show of it, knees aching and his back arching in a manner that's supposed to read as painful, when really, he feels mostly fine. Just a little dizzy, maybe. The symptoms could be psychosomatic.

"Okay," Olivia says, watching him walk into the other room.

This apartment is big enough for them both, though he did tell her that he doesn't know how much longer he'll be able to afford it. *Move in. It's better than living at home.* There wasn't much more to it than that. Olivia walked into this apartment with a bag. It's over there, on one of the dining chairs. Will closes the bedroom door, though doesn't lock it. Olivia seems to think about it. What are the chances that they stay close, but not touching, never touching?

Instead, she remains there on the floor, cross-legged, staring at the streak on her sleeve.

Breathing through her mouth, she whispers, "I hope so."

Forcing a cough, it comes out flimsy, obviously fake.

Olivia rests her head in her hands. Once again, shutting her eyes. She snaps into motion, instantly defiant of her initial choice to remain in the common area. On her feet, she paces around the apartment, eventually finding her perch near one of the kitchen windows.

When they first met… that's an entire story, one that begins with loss and goes from there. Her nails finally draw blood from her wrist. It takes her a minute to notice. When she does, she examines how the blood drips down her hand, in between her fingers. It reminds her of Will, the first time they tried. A little cut, nothing more, and take it in. It tastes familiar, slightly metallic. It looks harmless, sending her into a frenzy.

Olivia goes into the medicine cabinet, retrieving a thermometer.

Pressing the reset button, it beeps. She doesn't bother cleaning it before placing it in her mouth and she waits, the entire time staring back at her reflection in the mirror, never once breaking contact.

The thing about Will is that he always had one foot in and one foot out the door. Going to school for business, which then ended up with him majoring in accounting. He went along with every recommendation made that would position him for a higher tax bracket. Where did it get him? It got him a job as a financial advisor for a Fortune 500 company, a job that he obtained because of the various opportunities that go along with attending a prestigious school with an excellent reputation.

There's a whole lot that happens between graduation and his ninth year at the company, mere days after he turned 31, when it all came to light. A different kind of light. Think of it more like a burdensome blow. Will's the bored, restless, anxious type. He spends his workdays in a partial daze produced by medications he takes for anxiety. When those don't work, he has other pills to combat his paranoia. All through his tenure at the company, a company that he prefers to forget, never again to hear its name even whispered in passing, Will works hard, but never hard enough; he makes the cut, but never goes for the kill. It's all he can do to keep up what he's really doing, the scam that inflicted that heavy blow.

It goes something like this, based entirely on what little is left to be remembered, what little has been recorded. Most of the documents have been discarded, though Will's termination remains on record, something he can't duck, not now and not in another nine years.

"Hello?" It's a phone call from the secretary directing a call from the CFO. Odd because everyone in the company prefers email or text. "Uhh sure."

The CFO starts things off abruptly, making it clear that they both know what this is about. "I'm finding it hard to believe that you even thought you'd get away with this."

Will should feel something. He probably did feel something, the weight of the blow landing sudden and fierce. They know. They all know. Six figures redirected to a "mysterious" account. Money that wasn't his strategically stolen. All that money, perhaps thought to be put to better use, swiped, and used for, well, nothing much really.

Could it be that Will simply wanted the rush, the thrill of the take?

Why did you do it?

The CFO never bothers to ask. Instead, it's all by the book. The amount stolen, "It's upwards of $250k. Wow. I don't even know how…" After the sticker shock wears off, and it wears off quickly, the CFO paints the next 24 hours, the next 48, and then finally the rest of his life. "You can do some real jail time for this."

There is no version of this story where Will doesn't buckle and beg, and yet there's nothing he can do. He's in this alone.

Why isn't Chase, his confidant, the very same guy that conceived the loophole and worked with Will night and day, often chatting fondly about anything over the phone while he did his side of the transaction, Chase from the opposite coast, both at work during odd hours to make it all work... yeah, that Chase: Why isn't he mentioned?

Chase is never named because he is the one that reveals the details, framing Will, a petty little thing that wasn't anything more than Chase suddenly understanding the magnitude of the backlash and needing out *fast*.

When everything is on paper and reads of obvious deceit, Will is escorted by security guards into a conference room where he meets with people he's never met before, agents there to interrogate, cross-examine, and inevitably procure the full worth of this revelation.

"I don't know," he says, when they ask him why he did it.

After a few minutes of continued pressure, Will comes up with a better answer, "It seemed like a waste not to give it a try." Piques their interest, and it leads the investigation beyond what will become of Will and into the fatal security flaw that he (and Chase) had exploited to pilfer all those funds. By the conclusion of a single day, Will is washed up, though mysteriously given a pardon. No charges pressed, no jail time.

Afterwards he would wonder why. He'll never work again, not for any major company. They saw to that. When every job application begins with references, Will has only the one, and they would willingly sum up his character as "fraud, treason."

He won't ever fully know why he didn't end up in jail, and some days, especially as his savings continue to dwindle, he'll wish he had ended up behind bars. They used the information, the fatal flaw, to their advantage. Will all washed up, unable to show his face, his world shrinks from the office and the nightly happy hour at that bar down the street to his one-bedroom apartment and a steady diet of movies. That is, until he comes across Gerry, which leaves him so consumed and preoccupied, full body spasms and relentless shivers, painful vomiting and decimating lethargy. He doesn't come to, fully conquered, for over a month. When he does, it's like he's awakened from a nightmare, the world and everything in it suddenly quieter, less menacing.

He can only describe it as feeling "light," and it becomes the only thing he ever wants to feel ever again.

The thing about Olivia is that she never really had a chance. At age 25, she's never been able to be herself, going from parents that seemingly directed her every move, to a partner that had been initially so supportive, the love of her life, only to become a possessive and manipulative menace, effectively making her life a living hell.

There's so much that goes on behind closed doors, but all that can be discovered of her story is stripped from social media, discovered through old blog entries written mostly to herself.

They go as far back as age 15, entries that can only be retrieved using the Wayback Machine. Olivia describes herself as shy, but really, she just wants "to have friends that I can care about and that can care about me!" There's a lot of talk about being an artist but when she attempts to go to school as an English major, her parents forbid the path. "My mom says I'll be homeless in a day if I do what I want. She says that what I want is wrong. She slapped me across the face when I tried to explain to her how passionate I am about literature, maybe becoming a teacher. She tells me that I'm not talented enough. She says that I should study what I need to study. Life is about doing what you need to do to support yourself, not doing what you want."

Olivia's relationship with her mother is strained, but her interactions with her father are even worse. "I thought dad might understand because he taught history for like, I don't know how many years. Instead, he closed the door, told me to show him my writing. I was so nervous and didn't know what to show, but I had a few short stories that I had been working on. I chose to show him those. They need work yeah, I'm still learning, but he tosses them aside after a few pages laughing and then doesn't even care that I'm crying when he starts lecturing me about how tough the world is. Everyone's better than you, he tells me. Then he makes it personal and says that he didn't raise a failure and refuses to let his daughter descend into mediocrity. I try to defend myself, saying that it's my life and my dream. He sees it as me talking back to him and pushes me off my chair. I still have a big bruise on my left thigh."

Raised by strict principles passed down from generations of cutthroat parenting, Olivia grows up an only child and the sole obsession of her parents, every single iota of respect, as parents, coming from how well she does in school and in every extracurricular activity. So when she goes to school for computer science, struggling to pass any of her classes, Olivia decides that she'll go home for the holidays. Her body takes a few months to fully recover after the beating she receives from her father for not one but three Ds and an F. No amount of explanation saves her from physical punishment. Her second semester, the blogs become infrequent and really there's only one where she talks about how much of a rush it was skipping class.

The next blog is her fessing up with failing out of university. "It's okay. It's just not a life for me. I don't need it. I'm my own person. They don't understand. But he does."

It's the first hint of many that she has met someone. She calls him B, short for Bernard. They meet at a house party, and it's a real zero to 60, Olivia, so desperate for someone to understand and show her kindness. There isn't a whole lot in the blog about friends, save for her frequent mentions of having failed to connect with anyone. B comes around and suddenly he's all she writes about.

B is already working on his master's.

B works a full-time job on the side, his own resale business.

B plans to move to the west coast.

Everything looks great, Olivia working the resale business with B, eventually taking on a more active role. Somewhere amid the brisk and seemingly glorious relationship, they move in together. Approximately two months later, things begin to fall apart. B might be seeing someone else. B neglects her, continuously lies, lets his resale business flounder, forcing Olivia to run it all by herself. She's good at it, but when it's so much about maintaining professional relationships with various other resellers, she can't do much if they don't trust her. B hits her for the first time when she tries to confront him about a picture he posted on social media. It's with someone she doesn't know. A selfie. He says it's nothing. She doesn't believe him. The blog post omits what happens after. The next post is over a month later. There's no more discussion about B. She talks about how she got sick. It's all she can do to keep from being an unconscious husk of a person, drifting listlessly in bed. She makes excuses, saying all the cuts and bruises are from her illness. The blog goes silent for almost a year.

There are two more posts before the story reaches the current day. One consists of her talking about how she's turning 25 soon. "I feel weird celebrating it. Why am I celebrating the fact that I'm one year closer to death? What do I have to show for 25 years on this earth?" The next post is one sentence, "I turned 25 yesterday." From there, Olivia's story continues with her hospital visit, a bacterial infection. She is treated and released after 48 hours. Among the different instructions provided for recovery, she is given a brochure for a grief share group.

Olivia doesn't give it much thought at first. After a month of living back at home with her parents, both her mom and dad "cold shouldering" her, ensuring that in their eyes she is a disgrace, she needs something, anything that might provide an escape.

The grief share group meets digitally and physically, alternating weekly. Will goes to one in person but leaves after approximately 15 minutes, the entire time he squirms in his chair, unable to pay attention. People notice but it's not the time or place to judge anyone.

Olivia can't stomach the thought of being in a room with people, so she chooses a digital meeting. There are 46 people signed in, many of them with video on, everyone active in the chat.

Will tries the digital variety. The meeting begins with the moderator extending a chance for new attendees to introduce themselves. After a gentle push, people begin to speak up, unmuting themselves.

"Hi, I uhh," Will says, leaving his video off. "I don't feel comfortable showing my face. If that's okay."

The moderator maintains a soothing voice, explaining that nobody has to do anything that makes them uncomfortable. *This group is a zero-judgment, safe space.*

Takes a bit of courage but he introduces himself, stuttering a little, "I'm Will. I think I just need someone to talk to. Umm. Yeah. That's it."

There's much more to it, but language fails when put on the spot.

Olivia doesn't feel comfortable with audio or video, instead introducing herself in the chat. It's what she says, and how frank she is about it, that draws Will's attention.

"Hi, my name is Olivia and I feel trapped. I don't know how else to explain it. Like I'm ill, but I'm not ill. I feel trapped and I don't really know if I'm going to get any better."

There's a stream of people saying hello, the moderator acknowledging her chat intro, saying things like, "Grief can bring some of the darkest moments of our lives" and "it can feel like we'll never feel healthy again." It's a comment designed to help people, though perhaps people not quite like her. Or him.

He messages her directly, taking the chance. "Hey. This is weird. You don't have to reply. I just wanted to say hello. I think I get what you're saying."

Olivia replies instantly, "What am I saying?"

"You're sick," he says.

"I'm sick."

"But not like sick like a saying, or a metaphor. You're sick… like me."

She types something out, "I feel like hiding under my skin," only to erase it. Instead, she replies, "Are you sick?"

"Been sick for years," he says.

"Really?" She types the words, "That's cool" and again erases the sentence.

"Yeah," he says.

"What do you have?"

It's an answer that'll take the entire story to tell in full.

CHAPTER

11

This isn't the first time the landlord dropped by. He hasn't walked in, not yet, but that'll happen. It's inevitable. Will's been late on the rent for three months now. The bank account's got to be low, real low. Still, they manage to have food, getting out there daily to walk around and make sense of the day. Olivia doesn't really want to go very far, mostly because she starts to get paranoid, like somebody's going to see her. As if anyone is actually interested. Well, that might be true. Anyway, Will is more adventurous, enjoying the momentum of a walk and how it can put anything in perspective, no matter the circumstances.

"He's gone," Will says, peeking from behind a curtain.

"It gets scarier every single time he shows up."

"Yeah," he nods, watching the landlord get into his car and leave. Will's symptoms have faded. Donnie didn't even give him the weekend. He's well on the mend. Even the phlegm has let up, saliva coming in clean. The cough was gone in a day. "He'll be back."

"One day we won't be here," she says. How long has she worn that hoodie? It's been more than a couple days. "We can always try a different city."

"Yeah." He isn't really listening. His mind is elsewhere, already on the day's wanderlust. There's got to be another way. He needs a bigger crash, something that'll threaten to break him. Olivia too, though for the moment she's more interested in their upcoming homelessness.

"Maybe we can sneak over the border, up north. They got good homeless programs. We can get away from everything that we've ever known and start over…" Her musings continue, taking a familiar shape. She has talked about this before. Many times. It's like clockwork, the feeling of wanting to disappear. Will knows nobody will recognize them, not anymore. He's a felon. She's barely seen the world. The world won't even bat an eyelash in her direction. "They actually give the homeless apartments!"

He loves the optimism, but can't deal with it right now.

"Yeah…" He walks to the door.

"Are you listening to me?"

It's strange, what they've become. In the short time since they met and started talking, almost exclusively about his crashes, and subsequently hers, they have become inseparable. There's a strange bond forming, knotting itself around their individual lives, making it one unified form of codependency. They don't question it, because frankly anyone with half a brain can see that they need each other. They have no one else to turn to, and so they line up their brokenness and together maybe someday they can be one person.

The verdict is still out on that one.

Will reaches for the deadbolt, stops, and then looks at his hands. He turns to her, "How often do you think the average person actually washes their hands?"

Instantly, Olivia's mind drifts, a new quandary, something shared, "I… don't know. Like fifty times a day?"

He shrugs, "I bet less than that."

"How often do you wash your hands?" She follows his gaze to his hands. "They look clean."

"Only after I use the bathroom," he says. "Maybe I should wash less."

She sighs, "Donnie let you down."

"Yeah…" Still on the hands thing, but he finally looks up at her. "I think it's working."

By that he means what they've been chasing after. Nothing seems to really take them out anymore. Their bodies have crashed and each time it seems less and less, like their cells have become inhospitable to new viruses. No bacterial infections or diseases, nothing has brought them to their knees. Something needs to change. They are both getting worried, anxious, paranoid. The frenzy of a panic attack inches closer, and then all the memories start coming back. Memories can be murderous. How much longer until they think about it? Opting out is always a possibility. They wouldn't even need to be alone in doing it. He cuts her and she cuts him. They bleed pools until they're drained. Who would stop them?

"We need to try harder," he says. "I'm starting to feel… different."

She nods, "Donnie didn't even do anything to me."

"I'm sorry," he frowns. He opens the front door, afternoon sunlight pouring in. He grips the doorknob and then looks in her direction.

Olivia knows and says, "Why not?"

He kneels down, inching close to the doorknob and after a moment's pause, he licks it clean.

She laughs, "You're ridiculous."

"More like I'm desperate," he says. He makes a face. "Tastes strange."

"It's a doorknob," she says, walking over. "Move. Let me."

He stands back up, smacking his lips, the entire thing leaving him unsatisfied. Olivia takes her position and licks it twice, noticing that it's still damp from his mouth. She tries the door itself, seeing speckles of something, perhaps mud or grime. Afterwards, they go back into the apartment, Olivia pacing around the room. Will sits on the sofa, watching her. They are like this frequently, the aimlessness of their lives, the lack of a pursuit. Their minds are cavernous and full of monsters. She speaks up, offering a sample of what is currently in rotation within her mind.

"It kind of tastes the same," she says, eyebrow raised.

"What?" He doesn't seem very enthused.

"Oh, right, this one time, I was riding the subway. I don't remember where, probably to class. I was standing and holding onto the pole. There were people everywhere and I was doing what I always do when I'm stuck around people, holding my breath, concentrating on something, really anything, if it keeps me from fixating on the situation."

"I understand," he says. And he does. Will can't stand a crowd. It's like they're all talking about him.

"That's not it. It's that I was fixating on the pole so much and for so long that, well, I licked it. I didn't even realize I was doing it until someone next to me gasped."

"That's horrible," he sighs.

"People watched me as my tongue pressed against the pole, and it was still warm from other people's hands!"

"I've never licked a subway pole before," he says.

"It tastes the same." She pauses mid-step. "They all leered at me. I felt so ashamed. But not because of what I did. *They* made me feel embarrassed. I was the one that licked the pole, not them! Why do they care?"

"People feel entitled," he says, rubbing his forehead.

"Is the story upsetting you?" She returns to her pacing. "I can stop."

"No, keep going," he says. "What happened?"

"Nothing happened. I licked the pole, got off at the next stop, and those people were mean. End of story."

Will reaches for a bottle of cough syrup. She notices and says, "Feeling anything?"

He shakes his head, "We got to do something."

Olivia frowns, "I don't want to go out there."

"But nothing's going to happen if we stay in here," he says. He chugs the bottle, which will offer him nothing but a codeine high. Whatever gets you through the day.

By noon they are out of the apartment. They have not dressed to look well-kept. He wears the same pair of pants from who knows when and Olivia has the same shirt on, the hoodie taken off. You can still see the streaks on her sleeve. It's a warm day and they'll work up a sweat. That type of body odor is palpable and maybe it'll keep people at bay. They walk the neighborhood, which is mostly warehouses. He stops at a garbage bin and thinks about it.

"You go first," she says.

He reaches in, various discards, mostly takeout from one of the Chinese restaurants on the block, and he grabs a container. They aren't looking to eat spoiled food, they've done that. Amanda messes them up for an evening or two. They know what it feels like. They're looking for something else. Not sure exactly. But they're looking. That's the point.

He finds a plastic bag.

It had potential. Disappointed, he wipes his hands and he continues down the sidewalk.

Olivia remains near the bin, "Nothing?"

He shrugs, "It's not like we can see anything. But remember what happened with Amanda. I don't think we want to deal with her anymore."

She thinks about this, staring at the dried out noodles of uneaten lo mein and then catches up to him. There'll be more of this on their walk. They'll look at dumpsters and seek the hidden terrors of the outside world. At every street corner, they are unmasked and freely breathing in the energies of other people. It hurts to get close, but that's the only way they'll attract anything.

So they walk the more crowded sidewalks, easing into checking out different restaurants and bars. Eventually one of them will get an idea, something they haven't tried before, and they'll venture into a new establishment. Today, it's a pet daycare shop. They walk in, pretending to be customers.

"May I help you?"

Will speaks for them, "Just browsing."

That's not the right answer. There is nothing to browse except other people's pets.

"Excuse me?"

Olivia elbows him, "He means we're here to pick up our pet."

Will they pick anything up from an animal? It's possible.

"Oh, I see. May I see some identification?"

They're onto them. Still, you got to give them a nod for creativity. Olivia is able to get into the other room, hanging with the dogs, many of whom swarm her, showing affection, licking her face and mouth freely. They say a dog's mouth is cleaner than a human's, but in this moment, they're willing to try anything. The employees of the daycare haven't a clue who they are, and why they are here. It's more like they're suspicious of them potentially stealing a pet. But after Will shows them his ID, and they understand that they are not a pet owner, at least not one of their clients, they are asked to leave. By then, she's made contact and if there's anything there, they've taken that chance. Will apologizes, "I'm sorry. We were… confused."

Confusion isn't the right word.

Look at them. They seem like tweakers.

If only people knew what they were really after. Self-destruction comes in many forms.

Back on the street, Olivia is noticeably upset.

"What's wrong?" Will asks, keeping his gaze to the sidewalk.

"I want to go home," she says.

"Is it about what happened back there?"

Olivia keeps her pace, saying nothing.

"They thought we were messed up," he says. "Probably addicts."

To that comment she adds, "Who isn't an addict these days?"

Will looks at what waits for them up the street. A group of teenagers hanging on a stoop. They swarm the sidewalk. This could be bad. They look healthy. But they aren't thinking about contact. This could be bad in a completely social way.

"Careful," he whispers.

"Oh no," she winces at the sight. "We can cross the street."

"We could," he says. And yet, they don't slow their pace, the walk continuing, the distance between them and the group closing in until they are surrounded. The teenagers act like they don't see them, making it difficult to pass. In the face of others, Will and Olivia both deflate. There is no speaking up. In one instant, they go from standing there to pushing past the teenagers. That's sure to get their attention.

"The fuck?"

Their conversation is halted, all attention drawn to Will, whose shoulder went right for the center of one teenager's back. And then there's Olivia, tunneling through the gap Will created. Time seems to halt, and the group prevents Will from passing, forming a circle around them. Will still tries, another push, and then another, getting physical.

Something isn't right. Anybody can see that.

However, from Will and Olivia's perspective, they are trapped. These teenagers are tantamount to an attack. Their anxieties evoke odd behavior. Neither look at the teenagers. Their arms hang at their sides. Olivia starts to visibly tremble.

"What the fuck's wrong with them?"

The group is a blur. Will winces when one of the teenagers reaches for his arm.

"I'm getting creeped out, dude."

They close in, their curiosity aswirl, and yet this occasion is painted with bleak undertones. It isn't going to end well. The teenagers have no idea. When Will's provoked, he tends to lash out. Relatively scrawny, neither tall nor short, he does not look intimidating to anybody. Olivia even less, though they don't seem to pay her much attention. It doesn't stop her from forming a narrative, one that involves a group of male teenagers leering at her, threatening to take something, effectively vagrants seeking to steal whatever they have.

When she starts to cry, one of the teenagers backs away, frightened, "Bro, I'm out. This is way wacko."

Seeing an opportunity, Will sends his fist into the nearest teenager's stomach. The block erupts into chaos, turning heads, and resulting in even more attention. Will and Olivia push through and sprint away.

They don't stop until there are a few blocks between them and the incident. The teenagers don't chase, not that Will or Olivia notice. She trips at some point. Will doesn't realize but there's a gash across her forearm, the fabric of her long sleeve shirt torn.

They look at it and got an idea

She nods, "Best chance we have."

There's an urgent care near his apartment. It's been an object of their desire for some time, but they never got the courage to give it a go. The desperation has lengthened out long enough that they have no choice.

"I agree," he says. The incident fades into the background of their anxieties.

The urgent care is busy, but that's perfectly okay. They sit there breathing it all in. The sheer variety of ailments is intoxicating. Will and Olivia enjoy the wait. The waiting room is the best part. Why didn't they do this sooner? Waiting rooms in high occupancy clinics. Who knows what they might attract. Will becomes social when on the hunt.

"Tissue?" He offers the box to a young woman who is clearly feverish, her skin damp, glistening with the texture and luster that comes with higher temperatures. You can see it; just got to know what to look for. They're both pros at seeing the symptoms. Though it isn't anything they have known, it's promising. Everything here is promising.

"Thank you," says the stranger.

There isn't a lot of room for conversation in the waiting room. Will tries, gets strained replies, but manages to get someone talking in their direction for a few minutes. How many minutes does it take for the risk to increase?

People watching, they identify a Charles. The fever, the bloodshot eyes, the lethargy.

"I had that," she says, whispering in his ear.

He nods, "Same."

Eventually her name does come up. The nurse waving her over, "Right this way. Your boyfriend can come with too."

Anyone else would say something like, "He's not my boyfriend." Olivia is too nervous to say anything. She flashes a forced grin, showing maybe a little too much teeth, and the nurse is taken aback. In the patient room, they are left alone to feast on all the paraphernalia. Olivia remains seated while Will drifts across all the medical supplies, eyeing up what might be of some use. Eventually he finds it, the bin with the hazardous materials icon on it. He doesn't waste any time, reaching in and retrieving used needles. He pockets them with no concern, rather complete excitement, for how they might have been used.

Desperation, it's powerful.

"You'll be crashing soon!" he says, brandishing their score.

The doctor walks in and puts on the same typical show, "Good afternoon, what can I do for you today?"

Olivia is too nervous to speak.

Will comes up with something, "She fell and maybe has a concussion. I think she… is also feeling exhausted, maybe a fever?"

The doctor sits on a stool and moves around the room, grabbing supplies. "Wow, a bad tumble. Look at that." He gazes at her forearm. "Let's have a look, shall we?"

This is in no way fun. Olivia can barely stand all the human contact she receives from the doctor. He's in her face for longer than comfortable, holding her arm as he treats the cut, and then he forces her to put different devices in her mouth, only to come up with the most depressing of diagnoses. "Looks like you just had a tumble! No sign of fever or concussion, but I'd take it easy for the rest of the day. Kick back, watch movies, don't do any heavy exercise. You want your body to recover."

"Thank you," Will says.

The doctor considers the situation, and you can maybe imagine what could be a split second of suspicion, the two of them low on hygiene, high on anxiety. The doctor could call foul and see to it that they are examined in a very different way. But this is an urgent care, and there's a waiting room full of people. The doctor sees them off, wanting nothing to do with them, and in minutes they are back on the street, newly invigorated with their score.

Back in the safety of his unkempt apartment, they sit at the kitchen table, the needles splayed out and considered like crime scene evidence. The excitement is palpable, and when they make their selections, the needles stained with blood, they are sure to draw blood a few times, sharing the needles with each other. It's a form of intimacy, perhaps baffling to most, yet for both Will and Olivia, there could be no better moment of their day. They pull from their bodies and share what they hope will become another crash. Time will tell, yet the evening is bolstered with renewed confidence. There's even a moment when they get the energy to turn on the television, watch more than one episode of a show, before they are preoccupied with the same mutual fixations.

There are still more syringes to try out. It's enough to get them through the night.

CHAPTER

III

When it finally happens, they're too nervous to enjoy the upcoming crash. This is what they wanted, the onset of symptoms. It's like meeting someone new. There's fear there, folding into every action. They worry and they wonder what might happen. Olivia wakes up around 7 in the morning feeling dehydrated. She rushes into the kitchen, shouting Will's name until he stirs, roused to notice.

"I think it's happening!"

Will seems jealous, "Really?"

The thermometer hangs in her mouth.

"Here, your turn," Olivia says, handing him the thermometer. "99.7F."

He feels fine but uses it anyway.

Beep, the verdict is… 98.4F.

"It might take more time for you," she says, trying to make him feel better. "Everyone's immune system is different."

"Yeah," he says. He opens the fridge and pours himself some orange juice. "Tell me what you're feeling."

"I feel like I'm hungover, basically." She thinks about how to better describe it. "There's a slight throbbing, might be the onset of a headache. My mouth is dry, my nose feels itchy. Everything feels like it's been rundown, you know?"

"I do," he nods. He downs half the glass and then looks out the window. There's the ever-present worry that the landlord might be back today. Someone walks by and looks in the direction of the window. Will closes the curtains, afraid of being spotted. "You should go back to bed. It's easier to feel the symptoms that way."

She seems to agree, taking two painkillers. "Just in case."

It's not that they don't want to feel the pain. It's in many ways pleasant, especially when it's so all-consuming that they can think of nothing else. It's more like they take medicine because it's all part of the charade. Her headache will pierce through the veil that the dosage will temporarily provide. Popping those pills, it gets her excited. She comes alive, a skip in her step, as she walks into the other room. Will remains in the kitchen, brooding with disappointment. He picks at the fresh scab on his arm, a trace from the other night's syringe party.

Because there's not much else to do, Will lays down on the couch. He stares at the television screen, not bothering to turn the device on.

He falls asleep and wakes up gagging. Dehydration. Onset symptoms. His heart skips. There it is! There it is! He induces a cough, playing sick, and Olivia walks back into the room.

"Oh my god!"

He smiles, "Dry mouth, dizzy."

Naming the symptoms, it becomes clear that this one is Gregory. Their crash is on the horizon, and he gets in the same bed as her, the two of them taking their temperature again. The number has climbed, 100.5F and 99.6F respectively.

There's a palpable sense of comfort, knowing that they will soon be sick enough to fade into an unconscious haze. Theirs is a discussion entirely about keeping each other abreast of every feeling.

"I feel warm, and then I feel so cold. Freezing. It's getting worse too, not quite chills yet, but soon. I can feel the fever climbing. My voice also seems off, right?"

"Right," he says. "There's a little congestion."

"Tell me what you're feeling." She extends her arm, a mere inch away from touching his skin, but stops short. It's a gesture that's made to say, I'm here. I'm not going anywhere.

He nestles around her, spooning her increasingly sweaty body.

"Headache. It's dull right now but I can feel it getting worse." He seems to know what she'll ask next. "I'm not going to take any painkillers."

"It helps," she says. "Makes you feel the ache from a different angle."

"Naw, Gregory won't get the satisfaction," he jokes.

"Ouch, I just felt a pain in my temples."

"Your body is going to be very busy fighting Gregory off. I bet you'll have full body aches."

"Do you think we'll get any nausea?"

"Maybe," he says. "I'm hoping we come out in a rash."

Her eyes light up, "Have you ever?"

"No," he says. "You'd think I would at some point. I can't recall a crash where my skin showed the full extent of the attack."

"That's so crazy," she yawns.

"Go, sleep," he says.

"What time is it?"

He looks over at the clock on the bedside table, "Not even 11AM yet."

She's already fading. He sings to her, a light melody, something made up. Her breath slows, becomes heavy. Falls asleep. He aims to do the same. He sings to himself, staring up at the ceiling. It'll happen soon. Gregory will give them a hellish few days.

She wakes up screaming. Will's entire body jolts, springing to action immediately.

"What? What is it?!"

Olivia doesn't say anything, instead massaging her forehead. Headache has cut through the dosage.

He notices the sheets are damp. She's sweating profusely, her clothes equally damp. "Damn, you're really burning up."

The thermometer is back in her mouth, revealing that she is reaching 102F.

"The crash," he says.

Olivia can barely speak, "Fever, aches, chills, splitting headache, dry mouth… nightmares."

"Enjoy it," he says. He still exhibits just one symptom, headache. Tears well up and she tries to stand up.

"Don't."

"I need to…" She strips off her clothes, revealing her entire body. Will doesn't even notice, "Back to bed. You're probably hitting the peak."

He'll notice it later, when he's wide awake, watching her sleep. Her back will reveal a pattern of tiny red dots. There it is, worth the wait. A rash.

By then, he will feel the fever beginning to mount. Where she felt cold, his entire body will be on fire. He'll be unable to stay awake. Both asleep, they'll stay in bed until well after nightfall.

They don't have much of an appetite. At some point, she pisses herself. The complete loss of bladder control is something new. Will helps her out of bed. The circular pool of dampness is unmistakable. The same could be said for the smell. The atmosphere of the apartment has been tarnished, a sensation of complete unease coursing through every corner. This is the site of a tragedy unfolding and they are the stars.

He has begun to sweat, his shirt wet around the armpits. He takes off his clothes too. Knotted into his chest hair is a fragment of a potato chip. When was the last time he showered?

They lay side by side on the couch, the television turned on to a random channel.

"My body is confused," she says, her hand going south, between her legs. "I'm wet."

He looks down at his own genitalia, limp and unaroused. "I wonder what that means."

"I don't know," she groans. "But this is new."

The rash has spread across much of her body. He points to her chest, "Do they itch or hurt?"

She shakes her head, eyes closed. Gregory is sapping all her strength. "No. They don't hurt or itch at all. They seem to be just for show." Another groan. "My head, ugh it's pounding."

"Mine too," he says.

They remain on the couch, in and out of a fever induced sleep.

It's his turn to have nightmares. The contents are indescribable, but when he wakes up, he notices immediately the worsening symptoms. The rash starts on the webbing of his fingers, a tiny pattern of red dots. The headache makes it difficult to think clearly. He looks over at Olivia, who is still asleep. He watches her as she has difficulty breathing. An additional symptom to look forward to. He's on fire, his body drenched in sweat.

A rock-hard erection, he seems to be trailing her progress by mere hours.

How exciting. What might happen next?

Olivia massages her neck; the painful tremors pulsate with every heartbeat. She looks over at Will, who has fallen asleep. She sees that he has become suddenly aroused and though there is a lingering thought, not that they ever found each other attractive, more like she knows that there's other ways to transfer disease. The chase could be as simple as penetration.

She wakes him, "Have you ever, you know?"

He follows her gaze, "No. I've only had sex once."

"Oh," she says.

"What about you?"

"Nothing, yet," she says.

"Someday," he says, wincing. "Tremors."

"Yeah," she says, still looking at his erection. "The worst are the neck spasms."

"Gregory's really showing up," he says. He grabs his penis, gives it a few strokes and then stops. "Sorry."

"No, it's okay."

"Are you sure?"

She nods, "Yeah."

He continues stroking, a perfunctory act, the masturbation being absent of anything sexual and has everything to do with releasing what has become pent up. It takes him under a minute to reach climax. The sperm splatters across his bare chest. He doesn't bother wiping it.

"Your turn," he says.

"Okay." She sits up and spreads her legs. It takes her twice as long, a mixture of rubbing and finger penetration. The entire time, Will doesn't watch, fading back into a feverish sleep. He is brought back from slumber when she reaches climax, a single loud exhale. Olivia inspects her hand. It's damp with a clear body fluid. They make eye contact.

"Your fever," he says. "We should check."

First Olivia, 101F and then Will 101.1F.

"We're twins!"

He laughs, "I guess we are."

If they are twins, it is purely in the make and misery of their fractured lives. In both Will and Olivia, there is an idea of someone that had once been happy, been able to sit inside their body and not feel the frenzy that can only be silenced by contagion.

By nightfall, they are already beginning to tire of Gregory. The spasms don't last very long. The aching joints and body parts leave them both around the same time. Their fever remains, much like the rash. "You're right. It's for show," he says, inspecting his arm.

She sighs, "Yeah."

He starts itching the rash, hoping to aggravate it, make the most out of something that should have been more menacing. She seems to follow his lead, scratching her back. Really getting in there too, her fingernails leaving thin red streaks, cuts that would make anyone wince. Olivia breaks the skin, smearing blood across her back.

Congestion settles in, though absent is a cough. He snorts and swallows, but this is nothing like the others. It's barely cause for any lost senses.

Around this time, they begin to inspect the crash itself, and what it has become. Kind of like a review, they talk about which symptoms remain.

"I still have a fever, some congestion," he says.

"The rash," she adds. "There's that too."

"Gregory has been an afternoon," he muses. "But it's now evening and I'm starting to feel a bit different."

"Me too," she says. You can hear the disappointment in her voice. "Incubation didn't take long at all. But it's also a quick crash."

"I know," he frowns. "I would have hoped it would have been longer."

"This is the part I always hate," she says.

She stands up and does a few stretches.

He stares at the TV. "I'm always hoping it'll be the next one. The biggest crash… but then we get a string of minor strains, things that could never last longer than a few days tops. You could say I'm starting to get a little frustrated."

"It's this part," she says. "Right now, when I feel so light, like nothing at all can stop me. I know this is it, this is the delusion. It makes me feel so confident and so happy, but really what's happening is that I'm getting over Gregory. The details are the first to go, especially the particulars of the crash itself. They start to fade out and soon I'll feel everything. It'll feel the way it felt before. So many times before."

Will crosses his arms, sinking into the couch, "You know what I'm going to say next, don't you?"

"Ugh," she stomps her foot. "No, not tonight."

"We're going out. Tomorrow."

Olivia isn't happy with the reality of their situation and decides to take a shower.

Will remains seated on the couch; something on television catches his eye, the playback of a movie he's seen before. A man with nothing left to lose goes searching for the people that ruined his life.

"Isn't it always that way," he says to nobody, to himself.

After she gets out of the shower, Will switches places and cleans the layers of sweat and semen from his body. Olivia regains her appetite and goes into the kitchen, rummaging around in search of something to eat. The money is really starting to dry up because they haven't been this cleaned out since right after she moved in. She settles on eating untoasted wheat bread, scarfing down a slice in two bites. Afterwards, she examines the remaining symptoms. The headache is nearly gone. No more chills. Fever... it's about to break if it hasn't already. Olivia sits at the kitchen table, listening to both the TV and the shower running. She tests her senses, recognizing how sensitive they are when she isn't preoccupying them with a spiral of symptoms.

That's the thing about Olivia, even more than Will: She cannot be herself. Where there is a name, there is no real personality. Hers has been hidden behind years of hurt. Will might see moments when the real Olivia pokes through, but they are few and far between.

The Olivia that used to want to be a professor, an artist, is long gone. Her replacement is a person chasing a pain that will never be reproduced. Perhaps this registers plain and clear because she finally breaks down, a full-bodied sob, crying until the shower shuts off, letting it all out. The real Olivia shows herself during those tender minutes.

And then it's gone, wiped away by a tissue.

Will feels better and hates that he feels better. You can tell he's in a bad mood because he wants nothing to do with the latest plan. Instead, he buries his face in his laptop, scrolling around the internet, reading random articles, searching for... he doesn't seem to know. The most exciting part of all is when they feel the symptoms slacken and fade. There is no greater feeling than when it is clear that Gregory has been conquered. It's too bad that it doesn't last very long. It's nearly gone by the time he's out of the shower. He's really searching for something, like there might be something to gain from going on social media and reading about all that hate.

Olivia keeps her distance, watching TV.

Every so often, she looks up and checks to see if he's still seated at the kitchen table, the tapping and clicking of every keystroke.

He checks his email. Over a thousand unread, each bold headline having something to do with his treasonous past. One subject line just reads, "YOU PIECE OF SHIT." This used to cause so much hurt, loss of sleep and lack of any ability to think of anything else. For a while, Will read every single thing involving his termination, and each one was a devastating blow to his own well-being. Everyone saw him as a monster, and after reading enough of them he started to believe it. He probably is a monster. That's what made him go into hiding. He didn't leave the apartment for weeks. When he needed to eat, he ordered something, knowing well that he didn't have the cash flow for something so convenient. Yet, Will could not muster the strength to face the world. In his mind, if he walked out that door, everyone would stop and recognize him.

Look there goes that monster.

YOU PIECE OF SHIT.

Remembrances of that one article that fully outed his scam, whole emails that he wrote (to Chase) in confidence, painting a picture that proves he knew what he was doing. Another remembrance, how there was a petition to start an FBI investigation, in hopes that he would get jail time. The memories flood in the moment he signs into his email. For a bit, he takes pleasure in deleting each email, all left unread. He goes through pages and pages of emails. He stops on one that came from his sister. That one really hurt. Losing a family member, severing ties, is the sort of thing that can cause someone to kill themselves. He thought about it twice. The problem was that he couldn't even really get close to doing it. Even a razorblade seems impossible.

It all changed when he met Olivia. He doesn't even know what to call their relationship.

Friends? Partners? Confidants?

Whatever they are, it has certainly become a lovely and necessary thing. He wouldn't be alive if it weren't for her. The same could be said for Olivia.

He looks in her direction.

She doesn't seem to notice.

To be so vulnerable around someone… it's never happened before. His trust in others has waned, likely completely destroyed after the incident.

And no, he hasn't had any more suicidal thoughts.

He thinks about rereading his sister's email and then doesn't, the severity of her words is still too fresh. Really, you never get over something like that. The mere thought pulls him away, leaving him preoccupied. When he finally deletes the email, tears form in his eyes. His massive purge continues until he receives another email. The subject line is a simple "Think You Should See This." Wonder who it's from. The email itself carries only a single sentence, "A group of like-minded people and good conversation."

It's the kind of thing that would pique his interest. Will not Olivia, because he is more likely to take it at face value. Olivia would be more paranoid. She would consider it a threat. Funny how people exploit others by identifying what leaves them vulnerable. If you know what they have to lose, you can hurt them. Will, for example, doesn't want to admit it, but he still has something left to lose. It might just be her. She's watching TV right now. If Olivia leaves his life, what really is there left but a bridge, a noose, or a razorblade?

Another thought comes to mind. This link could contain a virus. It could contain a virus! The thought alone is enough to drive him to check it out. And that's all you need really, the temptation. What awaits you on the other side?

The Source requires a registration but when he finds out what everyone's doing there, he signs up instantly, exactly as planned.

"Hey, you got to check this out." The energy in the room shifts with the draw of a new source. The Source. That's what it's called, he realizes, and in mere minutes, Olivia is looking over his shoulder while he scrolls through user introductions. "Are they for real?" It's a question that is baffling considering who is asking it. Certainly, Olivia is too shocked to understand what she's saying. The server is split up into a half-dozen categories. Before anyone can post anything, they need to upload a profile picture, fill out a questionnaire, and post an introduction. The Source asks if they belong here. Will clicks on the prompt, "It's asking me to fill stuff out."

"I don't trust it," she says, her hand partially covering her face.

"I don't either," he says, going through with it. "We'll use a fake identity."

They are @FallsFargoHelp, profile picture is an image of a man mid-sneeze, found on a public domain image search engine. It asks for a status, and when they look for examples, it becomes clear: They are all chasers. Some mark their status "searching." Others mark their status as "symptomatic." There's one account that has labeled themselves "terminal." Behind every profile picture is someone providing details of their deadliness. This is how they both become rapt by the community. There are more like them. Better yet, if they all chase, perhaps they can provide an opportunity. Their latest crash was only a taste. There could be… no, there needs to be something more. They chase the lightness, twin images of people missing pivotal components of their being, where they need parasitic strains to latch onto their cells, becoming hosts to an invasion all its own, to feel anywhere near normal.

What is normal, really?

That's a question asked by the Source. They go with "searching" as their status and move on to the questionnaire.

"Normal," Olivia ponders the question. "Fear?"

"I don't think that's what they're really asking for," he says. Will is taking this really seriously. His body language is tense, back arched forward, his fingers sweating onto the keys. Olivia pulls a chair up, understanding that this has become the highlight of the evening. How can they move away from a moment like this?

There is no discussion about who sent the link. Normal here would be attempting to understand the source of the nudge. And yet, like new addicts, they sense the opportunity, and in the Source, they begin a comprehensive dive into a darker world.

"Normal is…" he says aloud, "being boring and thinking you're interesting."

"That's good," she says.

Next question: Are you sick?

They think about Gregory.

"I mean, I don't feel Gregory around anymore," she shrugs.

"It's already over," he sighs. "I don't even know what I was expecting."

She does, "A bigger crash. But it's never going to be what we expect."

"No, it won't," he says. Another sigh. "Okay fine," he types out the word, No. This is something they want to change.

Have you ever willfully sought self-destruction?

"Who wrote these things?" Olivia shakes her head.

"Moderators or whatever," he frowns. "I think I'm going to answer this question with another question."

"Ohhhh," she grins. "What are you going to do?"

"I think I'm going to ask, 'Do you ever feel like nobody understands you?'"

"That's good," she says.

The following question comes at him like crossfire, Have you ever had a sexually transmitted disease?

"Okay," he stands up. "I hate talking about sex."

"Oh come on, why are you so sensitive?" Olivia gives him a hard time.

"It just doesn't... it's just gross."

She points to his crotch, "That's gross?"

He nods, "Yes! It is. Sometimes it's like it has a mind of its own."

Olivia rolls her eyes, "Okay. Fine." Her turn to sit down and tackle the questionnaire. "I'll say yes. Even though that's not true. What the hell do they care?"

The next question asks about self-harm.

"I've tried killing myself a few times," he says. "I've mentioned that before."

"I know," she says, deep in thought. "I... used to cut myself, but I didn't really find it all that satisfying? I don't actually think I've harmed myself."

"Guess we need to think like normal people," he says, rereading the question. "A normal person would think we're very harmful."

"Way to be so perceptive," she laughs.

"I mean, just saying."

"I'm saying no. Because this place doesn't seem to carry those same values."

It's how they know what they're doing, how every name they come to know, and every crash they endure, every conquered battle that gives way to euphoria and confidence, they know. They know how unhealthy their lives are. They know this cannot last forever. At some juncture, a crash will take them. Perhaps the government will come knocking here to claim negligence, put them in a ward somewhere, lock them away where they can't harm anyone, including themselves. There's recognition, which makes all that manages to happen so very promising. The continued chase, the seemingly permanent desire that keeps them looking, the very same imperceptible drive that lures them into the Source, that is uniquely an affliction all its own.

They are sick.

What might they be carrying?

Dear patient zeroes, what do you carry in your bloodstream?

The questionnaire ends with one last question: Are you terminal?

"No," Will says instantly. A hint of regret. Olivia shares the feeling, looking up at him. They exchange a glance. She types, No, completing the questionnaire.

They get a welcome message that reminds them of the next, the last, hurdle.

Introduce yourselves.

"Why did you go with that screenname?"

Will doesn't want to say. "You know... because."

"Oh," she pulls back. "Right." Fargo. Fraud. A history that never fully heals. Will doesn't get to ever feel okay. They took that from him. Every day that remains will be veiled with a sense of malaise, paranoia, and doubt. Olivia carries her own depression, the feeling of being unable to understand why she can't stand being in this body, unable to see past the body dysmorphia, unable to retain any confidence unless she's feeling like shit. This feeling of being a waste, a wasted angel. They wear those outfits long after they've worn out.

"Allow me," she says, clicking on the intro tab.

Olivia takes the initiative, looking at some of the other intros first.

Hey my name is... I was diagnosed with... soon it became all I knew…

Hey my name is… I have a source… there's just nothing quite like it…

Hey my name is… just would rather feel this… I don't want to be alone…

Splayed across seemingly endless pages, there are introductions, many of them going all-in, fully heartfelt and honest, baring it all. They speak of the community motto, in sickness there is health. Their malaise gets dulled the more they are bombarded by physical ailments.

Olivia cracks her knuckles, makes a show of the entire thing. "I know just what to say."

This is her introduction:

"Hello, I'm Olivia."

Will warns, "Don't use your real name!"

"My name is generic."

"Still."

"Fine," she deletes it, starts again: "Hello, I'm Megan."

"Better," he says. "Sorry, but you just can't be too careful."

The point of an introduction is to be open and honest. Look at everyone and be judged.

"Can you let me just…"

Will takes a step back, "Sorry."

She takes a moment to form her thoughts. "I am happy to have found this corner of the internet. It's a lot like the city I live in where it feels so vast and scary and there's nobody that'll understand. I see that you all understand. I am on the mend and feeling better, but that's also the worst part. I don't feel right if I don't have a fever. It's like… it's like, when it's inside of me, it proves that I am powerful enough to fight. I can fight this. I can fight anything. I used to be the one that lost every battle. Some of you were strong enough to tell your full story, but all I can say is that this is very hard for me, opening up to strangers. It's scary, really. Anyone can be a monster.

Any one of you can see this, get ideas, and think about ways to take advantage of and maybe destroy me. That's what is so scary about the city, any city. It scares me into a corner. I am just happy I found this one! Please, don't hurt me."

The floodgates. When you post an introduction like that, it comes off so genuine as to become absolute vitriol for anyone looking to pick apart an already wounded individual. But you see, neither Olivia nor Will have this in mind as they watch the responses chime in, one after the other; their world is about as large as this one-bedroom apartment.

"Megan. Who invited you?"

"Think a city is scary? Wait till you see who lives in it."

"I think you might have the wrong server…"

"Megan, send pics. What do you really look like?"

"People hurt people, that's kind of the point."

One of the mods speaks up, "Welcome to the Source, @ FallsFargoHelp. Only you can see this reply. You made the mistake of replying all, leaving your introduction public. As the instructions stated, you should have posted to the mods, the appropriate corner of the server; otherwise, you attract the gamut of the Source's ire. Specific to this community is its anonymity. If you speak out, someone will respond. That being said, we do apologize for the mistake. We have deleted this introduction and provided you with a new username, @Renegades11Strain. Remember, introductions to the mods only. You'll want to say hello. They provide a wealth of experience, and many have been here since the beginning of the Source."

Will sighs, "Wow."

"I know," Olivia says, borderline speechless.

"Want me to give it a shot?"

"What difference does it make? Let's use my same intro."

"But I'd change…"

Too late. Olivia uses @Renegades11Strain and introduces

herself, again as Megan, this time to the #modmeet side of the server. The first mod replies, "Hello. Glad you got the directions right this time!" They don't give them much time to reply, "Everyone will say what they need to say, but I always like to help people through the darkness." They are sent what looks to be a direct invite. Do you accept? They seem so very mystified, yet because of what might be on the other end of this new venture, not yet a community, they both look at each other and decide to accept the invitation.

The server brings up a digital video conference room. Video is optional, and they decide to keep their camera turned off. The moderator appears to be a man with long hair, an oxygen mask attached to his mouth. The image immediately draws Olivia, who leans forward, cocking her head to one side. How curious, even Will wants to get a closer look. Olivia's paranoia drops instantly, replaced with an understanding that there is much more to what they've been doing, and perhaps they are mere amateurs.

"If you'll forgive me," the mod types. "I can't speak very well. I'm terminal and it has made it difficult to breathe, worse to talk."

"Of course," Olivia says. "I don't feel comfortable using video, or audio, if that's okay."

"That is perfectly okay." Then he introduces himself, "Kaz, I started this server two years ago with three other viral-affinites."

Viral-affinites, the Source's terminology for what both Will and Olivia call virus chasers. Here's a good spot to explain the origin of the term. A viral-affinite isn't necessarily merely a chaser; rather it's a living being, often a human being, that seeks out affliction. Far beyond Munchausen Syndrome, the viral-affinite is one that has taken the affliction, be it viral, bacterial, or "other," as a personal crusade. The viral-affinite sees the parasitic as a platform of power.

The origin of the term… well that should come much later, and from perhaps Kaz's own mouth. "We all had our reasons, but mostly we wanted to see if there was anyone else like us." He adds a smiling emoji, "Turns out there was."

"Two years," Olivia types. "So the Source is where we can talk about our crashes?"

"Crashes," he says. "Interesting term. We prefer to look at things for what they are. Call it whatever you want but here we see it as a journey, a part of one's crusade. We must leave behind a path of conquered afflictions along the way."

"How many have you…?"

"That's not a topic for right now. You'll likely meet others," says Kaz. "If you become ensconced into our community, you'll begin to see how deep a crusade can go. I'm here to say hello and to ask you about something sensitive."

"Sensitive?"

"Yes," Kaz types. "You see, this is an invite only server. We can boot you if there's cause to worry that you won't play by the rules, won't be a part of things."

Another shared look between the bond, the roles switched, Olivia becoming the one to continue engaging, "I want to be part of things."

"Olivia…" Will frowns, "I…"

"Shh, don't you get it?" She's whispering, as if Kaz can hear them. "The Source. It's what it sounds like. They are all crashing. Don't you see what that means?"

"Yeah," Will says, remaining doubtful. "But that means they might want something in return, and I don't know if…"

"We can always sign out. They are all strangers. They don't know us."

Kaz likes her latest reply and then says, "Good. Kind of like a step two of two for our questionnaire, we do need you to sign something."

"Sign something. That's kind of…" Olivia types and then stops, "Sorry. It's just not what I expected?"

"This server is unlisted. We remain confidential through and through. Still, what we do here requires a bit of trust. We like how things are run and we only want to bring in people that are willing to… play by the rules."

Kaz types incredibly fast, as though his words are instantly cast onto the screen.

"What must I sign?"

Olivia receives a document.

"Everyone that takes part in the Source, they must take the pledge."

The pledge. It's all in that document.

"Read through it," Kaz says. "I'll wait."

From the video feed, they can see how labored his breath has become. His eyelids grow heavy, and in the muted bright light of the room where he dwells, Kaz comes off as an apparition, the mere sliver of someone that had once held an active role in public life.

In full, every member of the Source must take a pledge: "They will sign in daily, updating both their status (attached to profile) and to post once in the appropriate section of the server according to their status (#searching, #symptomatic, #asymptomatic, and #terminal) a brief paragraph explaining the nature of their status on that day."

This pledge, the document goes into great detail to explain, Olivia skimming through the pages, telling Will what he might already understand. This is an operation. The Source is more than a community; viral-affinites are established. They are motivated; they are lexiconic. Why did they think they were in any way original? "If you do not update and post for 48 hours or more, the Source marks you as #terminated. Your account is forfeit."

"Well?" Kaz says.

They say yes. In the pressured moment, Olivia wants to see more. The thought of a bigger crash wins over the dulling effect of understanding that they are part of a subculture, a group of viral-affinites that knows so much more about strains and antibodies.

There was never any doubt in taking the pledge.

"Yes," says Olivia.

"Sorry, we need you to digitally sign the document. It's all set up; you can sign based on the username I assigned."

It all happens in two moves or less. Olivia is satisfied, even excited. Will has taken the brunt of the paranoia, yet after more mods offer their greetings, he too is lulled into a sense of calm and safety. After signing, Kaz quickly ends the chat, "Welcome! I'll let everyone have a turn." In minutes, other mods speak up, reacting to her introduction. Night and day, their replies are encouraging, some even offering advice right out the gate.

"Hey I'm Bert! I help moderate the conditionals. Welcome."

"Stacia. Nearly 9 months symptomatic. If I have any advice to give you it's to be a teacher, or work in a hospital. Easiest way to find afflictions. I've helped others with strains too. If you need anyone to talk to, I am around."

"I go by the name Jett. I hope you find use to our community. We take it very seriously."

They're full of questions and the collective mob of the Source's management entertains their questions. What they should have asked: What else is forfeit besides one's account?

Someone DMs their account, screenname @GetchLit00: "Go to #silence and read what happens when you're terminated."

Olivia finds the subcategory filed under #misc, and from there, every post that is marked #silence consists of cries for help. The accounts no longer exist, and yet there they are, a ticker tape of people calling out for help, with nobody in the community offering any response.

"I don't know what I have but I think I'm about to have a stroke."

"Someone's stalking me!"

"The rashes are oozing, and I feel sharp pains in my fingers."

"How can I save my son? I didn't want to give it to him!"

The one post that might have been enough to keep Olivia reading—"You all sent me there and abandoned me. Now my life is ruined!!!"—goes unnoticed, Will drawing her attention away with another suspicion, the thought that the landlord might be back, this time to kick them out for good. It's a whole charade that ends with Olivia going into the bedroom and hiding under the covers, Will watching TV until he passes out. The laptop remains open, screen darkened, until it goes to sleep too. The DM fades into the background, the #silence subcategory forgotten just like every single person and post marked as such, silenced for reasons that have everything to do with the Source finding reason to abandon a user, even if it means the Source itself going silent for good.

CHAPTER

V

Waking up without any symptoms reminds a person of everything they lack. Will feels every pain in his neck and back, the product of another night passed out on the couch. Olivia's eyes dart across the pockmarked ceiling of the bedroom, the mattress still odorous from Gregory, creaks as she turns to her right side, unwilling to face the day. The clock on the bedside table announces that much of the morning has already passed. Will massages his neck, the first to stir, climbing to his feet to check and make sure nobody is outside. The landlord, he could be nearby. Today might be the day. During these lucid moments, one must imagine Will almost begging for the eviction. Just make it happen. The wait often becomes its own brand of torture. And yet, nobody. There's nobody here, or perhaps it's more like whoever's watching, Will can't see them.

He goes into the kitchen, reaches for the nearly empty tin of instant coffee, and works on filling the kettle. At the table, he eyes the dimmed screen, The Source teasing him into checking in. They made a pledge. There will be a status update.

Olivia calls him from the bedroom.

"Will…"

He taps a key. Couldn't resist…

Cursor is still pointed to the server, though it forces him to log in. "Yeah?"

"Will…"

"Hey, what's the password again?"

He doesn't get an answer, Olivia beckoning him to join her in the bedroom.

"Fine," he says, sliding the chair away from the table. In the bedroom, he sees the same image, Olivia on her side, eyes slightly unfocused, the depths of a sincere and decimating depression have claimed her overnight. "What… what was the password?"

"Will," she whispers.

"What? I'm right here," he says, clearly frustrated. Right about now all he wants to do is sign into the Source, the act still so fresh, an unknown, it compels him to make a good first day, a first impression, the introductions last night feeling more like an interview and this, it's the first day on the job, first day. Nobody ever wants to be seen as something they're not, even if they so desperately want to be left alone.

"Will, I…" She fakes a cough. "I feel…"

"You're, what?" He snickers, "You're not crashing."

She gags, "But I…"

He reaches for a pill bottle, checks to see how many are left, and then says, "Yeah, you're not crashing. I get it. You're feeling heavy."

"Will…"

"Things are feeling heavy," he says, "but we got to keep with it. We made a pledge. We can't just bail on it now."

"Why…" Olivia with another forced cough. She checks the crux of her forearm, perhaps hoping to see some evidence in her saliva, discoloration where there should be none. And there is none, her skin dry.

"You are the one that did it!"

"You want to impress them," she says.

"That's not true." Anyone could see that it's true. Will wants to impress. A new social opportunity that just might sweeten the odds of their own chase? His mind obsesses over the chances.

Olivia turns away from him, sinking deeper into her depression.

"What the fuck?" He can't quite believe her mood this morning. "So that's it?"

"helpmeimsick," she says.

He doesn't quite hear it, "Huh?"

"h e l p m e i m s i c k."

The password.

Now here's the fun part: Does he stick around, or does he rush back into the kitchen so that he can get involved with the affinites? A person has their own interests to protect, but in navigating any bond, there is a certain tertiary transaction that comes with maintaining the bond the longer it is held. It's why so many people keep it "strictly business." They hold onto a friendship until either they receive what is desired or things begin to flounder. Stick around after any agenda is redeemed and a person develops a shared history. If there's history, there's information to fall back on, becoming an absolute mess.

Will, it seems, is a mess.

He demonstrates some compassion, sitting on the edge of the bed, "Hey, what is it? I don't understand. We should be motivated."

"What does it matter?" Olivia talks into the blanket, causing Will to lean forward, his body pressing against the blanket, the weight enough to send the wrong signals.

"It does matter," he says, voice soft, an attempt to appear tender, and caring, when really he might be doing this because he simply cannot do it alone. "Maybe you're just overwhelmed."

Olivia remains silent until he notices that she has fallen asleep.

He mirrors her motions, scanning the disrepair of the ceiling, checking the time, navigating the frustration of the current moment.

"Well," he says, standing up from the bed.

He has the password. Time for a status update. Logging in is easy enough. Remembering to continue pretending to be Megan (@

Renegades11Strain) proves to be much more difficult. He switches status to "searching," and proceeds to go to #searching and types out the following update: "We're alive and inching towards normal. We don't really feel comfortable at this juncture. We just got over Gregory, but that was a 24-hour thing. It went by and Olivia and me, we're getting really hung up on this low point, where we don't really feel much of anything and we're both paranoid and depressed, taking turns battling both. It's just that we're searching. Yeah. We're searching." He hits send, the post going live. We. Olivia and me... He recognizes the negligence and frantically searches for an edit function. Good thing nobody reads these updates. Nobody that would take advantage. The mods may have noticed, but they can rollback every single edit regardless of any deletion. All they need to do is look.

He has a mini-freakout, finds the edit function, and fixes the error. A tragedy narrative for one, consolidated across a three-and-a-half-minute runtime.

Megan. He must post as Megan.

They have satisfied the pledge. Will is free to explore the Source. He ventures into new corners, finding #toldyouso, a subcategory that is managed by Stacia, a mod that he recognizes from last night's interactions. Seems members use this area of the server to make predictions and bet real world currencies on everything from the judgment of others to the spread of various afflictions. That's one thing he has already noticed about the Source: Every act is based around being a viral-affinite, meaning all is compartmentalized into the act of measuring another person, animal, anything for what they can endure.

It might have been refreshing if Will didn't already feel so judged.

Stacia is active, in conversation with two "subordinate" members. Will notices the level of a member is based entirely on how long someone has been active. Both have been a part of the Source for at least six months.

Stacia upvotes Harley's comment, "Derf was terminal. He lied about it because he refused to give up."

Harley likes that Stacia upvotes, validating the choice to provide another comment, "And I'll have it be known that I bet a nice figure that he'll be gone in a month. Nothing speaks louder than cash."

The other user, Monk, is in defense of this Derf, "It's kind of heartless to assume that he's lying. He's a liar because he stopped updating? Maybe he had enough of the toxicities of this space."

Downvote.

Stacia offers a warning, "Everyone's entitled to their own opinion. Don't claim the entire community as suspect. We are talking about Derf, nobody else."

"Right," says Harley.

Will is a bystander, watching as Stacia raises the stakes, offering motivation for the two to face off in a debate. "If you're confident, let's ante. Wagers?"

"+100," suggests Harley.

Monk counters with a "+50."

Stacia meets them in the middle, "I don't want to waste too much time on this one. +75."

There is mutual agreement.

Will is slumped over, watching the entire scene unfold with equal amounts of fear and fascination. It is in every way a fight where nobody wins, and everybody involved is too close to see beyond the wager.

Harley offers some screencaps, Derf having been at least somewhat friendly with this user. The images reveal that Derf had indeed been hiding his condition. The reasons for this are far less interesting for someone like Will than the symptoms, which Derf thankfully disclosed—a full body rash, high fever, chills, congestion, delirium. The worst of it is in the second to last screencap, an image of the culture of cracked and dry skin around his mouth, and all other orifices, as though every natural opening and orifice of Derf's body had become irritated and infected, causing them to ooze with yellow pus and break out in painful sores. Will lingers on those images and eventually saves them to the laptop.

Returning to the debate, it appears that Monk must have experience in the court room because they provide an expert analysis, offering possible afflictions cross referenced by location and spread of the strain.

"How much did you make off Derf?" Stacia asks.

Harley is less willing to disclose this information.

"That's no fun," she says, giving Harley's reply a downvote.

"Fine. Fine, here." Another image, this with some account information blurred out, but it looks like a p2p pay app, latest transaction netting +5,910.

"That's a heavy penny," Stacia says.

"I would lean to there being some insider trading going on here," Monk offers, following their reply with a request for email exchanges.

Will takes a step back, triggered by the mention of insider trading. It calls back his own missteps, the bulk of which still weighs heavy on his entire, almost infinitesimal life. Once upon a time... Will clicks away from the debate unfolding and moves back to the main categories.

You can't run away from it.

Worse, there's nothing to distract, nothing to battle and destroy. Will has nowhere to put down all his hurt, no one to give it to. The immediacy of feeling so exposed, he runs through all the options. There aren't many. There's an unsuspecting Olivia in bed; he could direct it all onto her, or he could go back into the Source and find something to interject his anger, his frustration, or it comes down to more of the same: He pours himself a cup of coffee, chokes on its harsh taste, and keeps scrolling. He pauses to listen. The landlord? Someone else?

The wonder...

Paranoia spikes in accordance with the caffeine.

Will gets a notification.

One tab is highlighted red, #incoming. Among the dozens of categories and private areas of the server, this one is run by Kaz, the very same person that screened Olivia last night. The notification must have gone to every member of the Source because Will enters #incoming to an overwhelming conversation. The up and downvoting system makes it easier to navigate, though Will can't quite keep up at first. From a distance, he's the new user, slowly understanding what this is. It's what the Source does best. #incoming was one of the first categories and the main purpose of launching the server. Kaz runs it all on his own, opening conversations when he sees fit, and particularly when there is something incoming, a new outbreak.

Kaz's pinned post reads simply, "Roanoke. Last 72 hours, +80 hospitalized. Situation critical in those infected. Roanoke locals: unadvised. Source: @Olighaz_1, med tech, status: symptomatic."

It will take Will some time to understand. What is there to understand? The thing about the Source is that it does not sit still. Unlike other interest groups, the Source is built around a hive mind that involves finding opportunities. The viral-affinite needs the next affliction. It was built on selfish needs, and here, as Roanoke is picked apart for all possibilities, members react like animals around a fresh kill.

@Olighaz_1, also known as Max, is second to Kaz in the ongoing discourse. Kaz explains that the affliction is likely to be a more aggressive form of influenza. "These sorts of strains spring up quickly and then die out because they are so deadly, the CDC sends their specialty units out to the site of patient zero post-haste. Max, will you?"

Max provides additional details using a video stream. He wears a white lab coat, wearing glasses, and speaks with a prolonged drawl. "It's going to be contained," he says, with confidence. Roanoke's onset strain will likely infect 100-150 people before those infected are either "taken care of" or pass away. "They've already been quarantined," Max says.

"How do you know this?" Kaz enters the video chat, preferring to speak via text. "How sure are we that this is merely a spurt instead of an outbreak?"

Max thinks about this and then says, "Because the CDC was here before anybody even knew. I was in the middle of yesterday's shift, feeling dehydrated and didn't know why because my status was searching, nothing recognized. Suddenly we get bombarded with calls and a unit of four shows up telling us what we need to do. Telling us, not cluing us in."

"A spurt, then," Kaz says. "This means it's manufactured or it's reactionary."

Max nods, "Manufactured. That's what I'm thinking."

This is the part where someone like Will, who is still so new to the culture of this cutthroat community, and more so the industry surrounding biological ingredients, might become even more paranoid. Suddenly it goes from nature being the impetus of an affliction to the possibility that people are buying and selling, engineering and testing, orchestrating whole narratives around the spread of a strain, for reasons that almost always come down to an opportunity, one that when measured is worth the risk and usually yields lucrative results.

A revelation just as often comes across as revulsion.

Worth wondering how Will might take in the weaponized and capitalized nature of the Source, including its integrated sources. For now, he is an armchair user, watching and reading as power users and mods stir the Source, expertly building their next move.

And they are indeed going to move.

"That's my worry," Kaz says, responding to the prediction. "Manufactured means it won't last as long. It could already be null."

Max shakes his head, "I don't think so. 80 have been hospitalized and most were admitted around the same time. I've been keeping focused on their progress. They are exhibiting all the telltale signs of Penthurst, only expedited."

Penthurst. A spurt that happened last year, a form of influenza that resulted in nine dead and 131 total infected. The strain was manufactured, and though the culprit was never found, leading viral-affinites to believe it was a governmental test, it lasted 48 hours and the Source sent an all-hands alert to any that might be able to make the trek. Many did, though they are not reported as part of the 131 infected. Affinites keep their status internal, collected for personal use. Penthurst happened and nobody noticed. Media suppressed because the media never knew about it.

"Expedited," Kaz notes. "What are we looking at?"

Max doesn't know. He can only postulate, "Tomorrow. That's the window. Now until tomorrow."

Kaz pushes buttons on his end and soon the thread collapses, and the information is parsed into a single post, pinned to the top of #incoming.

The details in plain:

"Roanoke. Ticker – 10 hours. Suspected manufactured influenza. Fast acting, affliction likely to pass in <72 hours. Close contact necessary. R=2. Affinites gather. Approval necessary."

Approval necessary.

Will reads the details multiple times. He writes them down, his penmanship jittery, difficult to read, even for him. He no longer has a steady hand, though it isn't from too many crashes. When was the last time he ate anything? If he noticed, he'd understand that it's been almost an entire day.

No details regarding approval are provided. Will moves through different tabs, returns to #incoming, and rereads the pinned post for a fourth time.

This is it. He can quite literally see the haste and excitement across all members. He's witnessing the Source in full effect. Members are posting responses to the pinned post, a confusing blend of emojis. There's a purpose to every chain, but Will does not possess the key. The emoji streaks are succinct means of providing critical information about location, time, and other details involving planning. After a few incidents where members targeted other members, personal details have become codified through emojis and additional private DMs.

"Newbie. You won't have a lot of time. Roanoke, VA." There's an attached photo depicting a map, the general area, and the street address of the hospital. "Can't and won't tell you details about gathering bc don't trust you."

"Can you at least tell me when, what time?" Will asks, desperate for some clarification.

"No, my job here is done."

What Will can never know is that the anonymous tipper was Bert, one of the mods. His job is to fish out the new accounts, giving them a passing chance. Someone did that for him, long ago. It became an act of community service. Every community has its culture, and Bert, you see, he was one of the people that made things happen, got people together. When some people were targeted by other members, attacked without warning for reasons having only to do with some viral-affinite's obsession for affliction, willing to take a life if it meant ensuring procurement, it was Bert that felt the sting of the community's failure. There were few policies back then, and only a handful of mods. Bert took it hard. He blamed himself for the losses. Nobody tells him to go down the list of new accounts, encouraging them to take part. That's all him. How ironic, then, to know what this looks like: Someone hoping to do good, help others, does not realize that by providing clues, he leaves them ill-equipped. They are told where, but not how; what but never who. There is half a transcript, illegible when seen in full. But for someone like Will, and certainly for Olivia as well, the desperation fills the blanks. It reads like a guarantee.

Tomorrow, they'll be able to crash.

Olivia emerges from the bedroom, "I don't want to live this way."
Will looks up from the laptop, busily taking notes.
He grins, "We don't have to."
The Source provides.

CHAPTER
VI

Life is a series of important lessons. Among them is one regarding people. People will always let you down. A disappointing discovery for many, yet for Will and Olivia, they put themselves out there only so often, a real rarity given all that has already been endured, so when they try one more time, and it doesn't play out as expected, it's a lesson repeated, a lesson so hurtful they'd perhaps ready themselves for the final and definitive departure from society.

How it plays out is that Will tells Olivia all about Roanoke. They only have the day, barely the night, to make the trek. Travel? It's out of the question. Their wallets empty, how can anyone, much less two chasers like Will and Olivia, make the 8-hour trek to the east coast?

Figure it out.

"This could be our biggest crash," he tells her. He won't take no for an answer. It's not great, Will getting desperate, layers of would-be compassion peeled back as his senses recover, and every single demon comes knocking, preying on his paranoia.

"I know, but it's impossible," Olivia says, turning away from him. He hasn't stopped arguing since the Source sent the notification. "I don't think we can make it in time."

"We will," he pleads. "We will!"

The way this looks, it's something familiar, which is telling of modern-day social intimacies, the dynamic of one striking dominance over the other due to a blend of gender stereotypes and physical strength. Theirs is a unique bond, built on the same demons that have since come out to prey. Look at him, this is why he did what he did. He just can't help himself. An opportunity so clearly on the horizon, Will won't take failure as a possibility. He needs to take it before someone else does. Olivia cowers in the face of his belligerence, the constant goading and coercion, "Look we can make it work. I've got… in the bank… and this place is going to be repossessed anyway… and… and… and…" It never ends. He won't quit. Anyone would get tired of his continual blabber, and eventually Olivia broke down, tears et al.

And he still won't quit.

He knows what he wants.

Perhaps she might see what she's gotten herself into, except that's not in the cards. The deck is rigged, and her hand is webbed with his. There is no going back. Will is the least hurtful, and yet hurts her all the same. It runs in one's bloodstream, buries itself in one's brain, all the same. She can't control herself, wilting like a dead flower into the couch cushion.

"And… besides, you trust me, right? You trust me! Come on, right? We got to do it. We got to. And… and… and… It's not like you have any better options!"

There it is. When persuasion becomes activation: Will touches her, grabbing her arm because he's frustrated. She doesn't seem to be listening to him, freeing her arm. "Don't touch me!"

Will doesn't apologize, too determined to change her mind, "Look… it's either this or… and besides…" It's a dizzying ramble, a one-sided argument. The words often run together, and one might even suggest that Will could have dosed himself with something, yet it's more like he's on no sleep, wired and tired, and more so fixated on how there is a "surefire" acquaintance, just 8 hours away. Just 8 hours away and he could be crashing harder than ever before.

Anything. Do anything. Whatever it takes, just no more feeling like this.

It's selfish, what he does next.

He tells her, "You're nothing without my lead."

Olivia sobs. There's nothing to say.

She's going with. Every cell in her body tells her it's going to be a disaster, yet from years of being told she was less, beaten by dad, beaten by boyfriend, berated by mom, being told, the same thing day after day. You're nothing. Nothing at all without _____. Something breaks, and the contamination buries itself into that fresh wound, an infection that will spread through a person's entire body.

"There's a bus leaving soon," he says, pulling her off the couch. "We can make it in time."

They get to the bus station, waiting around the corner until the driver looks the other way, chatting on the phone and smoking a cigarette, to sneak onto the bus. They've never done this before, but it's remarkably easy. Perhaps they aren't the only ones that steal a seat. When the driver climbs up those steps, sitting behind the large steering wheel, he mumbles into the microphone the usual introductions, the bus to Blacksburg. It's full, not a single seat unoccupied. This is a point of anxiety for Olivia, who sinks into her seat, thankfully taking the window. The stranger next to her keeps to himself. Will had the idea to spread out, her near the back, him near the front. If they're together, they're more likely to be spotted. Not a bad idea, though Will likely decided to sit away from her because he played out the scenario in his head and there is a chance Olivia might crack, believing that she might ruin their chances. Nothing worse than getting kicked off the bus between destinations.

She concentrates on her breathing, her focus only on the road. No eye contact.

Will sits in the aisle seat, third row. He stares straight ahead, as if he's the driver, watching the vehicles navigate the lanes.

An hour passes, a smooth ride. The cabin is mostly quiet, the occasional passenger on the phone, or exchanging a brief back and forth with someone next to them.

Olivia begins to feel nauseous, the ever-present blur of asphalt at high speeds causing a whiplash effect. She dry heaves, the person to her right, their reaction is alarming. Instead of telling her to calm down, or to be quiet, they offer to help, "Ma'am, are you alright?"

Making eye contact with a stranger… deadly business. There are two things that she notices: 1) this person is unnaturally kind and 2) they are wearing a mask. Another observation, everyone is wearing a mask.

"I'm…" she takes a breath. "I'll be okay."

"I get car sick too," the stranger says, they have long brown hair tied into a bun, heavy eyeliner around their eyes. "Buses tend to be worse. It's the axels, the size of the wheels, and that up/down motion. Real queasy," they gesture to their stomach.

Olivia holds her breath, nods, doesn't feel any better.

"Where you headed?"

There it is, people seeking answers. People wanting information to frame a stranger into a container, make sense of their worth, hang them up on a wall like a picture frame, as if to say: You are this and I get what it is that you do. What does Olivia have to say that isn't a lie, something conjured out of thin air to keep this stranger from knowing anything about her?

"I'm headed to… Blacksburg," she says.

"Ah, end of the line, I see."

"Yeah," Olivia says, holding her breath. Exhale. Feels the same. Nerves get in the way too, and now she's started up a discussion.

"I'm headed to Richmond," they say. "Visiting family for the holiday weekend."

It's a holiday? Olivia doesn't quite understand their statement, instead moving on with the niceties, "That's great. Yeah."

"You could say that," they laugh. "It'll be stressful but hey, it's family."

Family, no filter. A family member will call it like it is, because there's very little in the way of being penalized. They'll look you over and tell you things like, You've gained weight. You look older. Deeper the cut: Why couldn't you be someone else, someone better?

"Yeah," she tries to match the same level of laughter. Then it catches her eye, a second time. Recall the mask. "Should I be... umm?"

"Oh," the stranger shakes their head. "Not going to judge. I hate that people are so judgmental. I'm just being careful. I got to travel a lot this month."

"Is there something going around?" Olivia asks, her interest piqued.

"When is there not?" The stranger says, and then adding, "No I'm joking. But seriously, it is kind of scary right now."

"Yeah, it is," says Olivia.

"The fact that another strain of Covid is going around is so ridiculous," they say. "Like, when will it ever end?! I've had it twice, but then I start seeing on social media people saying that the new strain going around, I forget what it's called, it's some number jumble, is scarier because it's like when it started, all those symptoms, and people that have it are getting the bad brain fog. I can't have that brain fog! If it affects my brain, and I get stuck with that fog for months, I'll fail out of my doctorate. It's really life or death."

Olivia stares at the mask, "You can't be too careful."

"You really can't. These viruses have the upper hand. I had a friend that got sick and was hospitalized. He never recovered."

"He...?" She teases out the information.

"Died," the stranger nods. "It was horrifying. I can barely talk about it now. My point is this world makes us think like we're strong and powerful, the top of the food chain, and then a virus comes in and shows us that really we're outnumbered. It's what I'm studying."

"What is it that you're studying?"

"I'm studying to become an epidemiologist." They look around the cabin and lower their voice, "But don't tell anyone."

"Who am I going to tell?" Olivia grins.

"It's just something you say," the stranger says. "What do you do?"

The question changes the entire conversation, making it awkward. Olivia goes cold, coming up with an obvious lie, "I'm a... social employ—I mean worker. Social worker."

"Ah, I see."

Olivia turns, facing the window. There will be no more banter, the stranger continuing to be a stranger, perhaps taken aback by the sudden cold shoulder, but like any social cue, it is dealt with and those within the dealing take notice. In this case, the stranger goes back to their devices, doom scrolling between emails answered, and Olivia stares out the window, watching the trees blend together, the steady stream of vehicles pushing 70MPH in hopes of reaching their destinations.

Outside of Richmond, the bus pulls into a rest stop. The driver announces, "We got an hour here. Be back at exactly 5:30PM. Don't be late or you'll be left behind!" Both Will and Olivia remain on the bus, among the last to deboard. It's interesting to see how Olivia stays put, too fearful of what might be out there. Will checks on her, but is too on-edge and worried that they might be spotted to walk over to her seat, so they exchange a single look before he gets off the bus and walks around the rest stop. People are indeed masked, an indicator of something big on the horizon, which excites Will into seeking adventure. He stands at the front door of the rest stop, watching vehicles pull into parking spaces, people spilling out, counting the masks. Keeping track of every cough and sickly sight. A line of eighteen wheelers occupy the western edge of the rest stop, truckers in a frenzy, walking to the rest stop and using a separate entrance. Will tours the area, observing the humanity of just another rest stop, another transient location where people rush to enter and rush to leave. This is perhaps where something might linger, waiting to catch a ride. He'll see what others wouldn't care to see. And it's more than a wayward cough, droplets airborne as a family walks right into the cloud, a pairing made that won't be visible until days later, when the family starts showing symptoms while on holiday; it's more than the grime underneath one's shoe, the undergrowth of affliction of which the viral-affinites keep a delicate measurement. This is about transaction and exchange. There, it's right where you are, if you're looking. Will sees a young man, standing idly near the trucker entrance. The way he takes a half step forward, a quick verbal exchange between trucker and the young man, but only when it seems right, that's a tell. It indicates a transaction of a different sort, one that compels Will to pursue. He walks up, stands next to the young man, as if ready to mimic his transactions.

"$50 a blow," the young man says, after a spell. "$25 if you just wanna watch."

Will might play ignorant, but where's the ploy in that? He wants it, not the sex, and certainly not the release. He sizes up the young man, and it's every bit like trying on a shirt, seeing if it fits. Will can sense the possibility, something he and Olivia have talked about. What's another item crossed out? They tried the needles, now it's time to go fishing, deep throating for another name. Who might he meet?

The fact that Will doesn't back away, it's enough indication for the young man to lead the way. "There's a private spot around the back."

Will follows him to the loading dock, the steel shutters closed. The young man unzips and is already hard. "Let's go," he says. It's just another transaction.

Licking his lips, Will lowers himself, the intimidation fading as he tentatively takes the tip into his mouth. There's an odd taste to it, but it passes, and soon it's flesh in his mouth, the motion quite familiar, and with his eyes closed, Will is able to get through the act without too much resistance. The young man stands there, like a prop. There's nothing to this, zero emotion and absolutely no feeling. Will hopes that there's something new in the warm liquid that comes out of the young man's climax, a possible plan B if Roanoke offers nobody new. He hopes, and in that hope, this isn't him getting a stranger off. This is tantamount to trying something on at the store. Eventually it'll be worn. He just needs to wait for the right occasion.

Back on the bus, Will returns to his seat. He can still taste it. Taking a sip from the coffee he bought afterwards, he can only hope it'll be enough to quell the aftertaste.

Maybe they don't think Will and Olivia are good enough. When they arrive in Roanoke, the members of the Source are already mid-action. The server tab #roanoke is active, seemingly hundreds of posts acting as a livestream of where they are, where they'll be, and where things will become ground zero. It's supposed to start outside the hospital. Will and Olivia stand out front, eying everyone that walks inside. An ambulance pulls into the drop-off zone, sirens blaring. Two EMTs tend to the gurney, the person laying on it already strapped to an IV. Record timing with their unload, rushing into the emergency room in under a minute.

"Wow," Olivia says, amazed at the sight.

They watch as a car pulls up, the driver helping the passenger to their feet. It seems like perhaps they have been cut, an accident, because they limp along, holding their chest. There's blood streaked across their arm and shirt.

People watching is all fine and well, but something big is going down inside that building. They made it in time, so then where is everybody?

"What's happening?" Olivia asks.

"I don't know," says Will.

The Source tells a different story. Members clamor over a supposed altercation with a nurse. One user goes on to call out Kaz, "Can we get some help?! They're calling the cops!"

Amid the fury and the heat of the moment, the mods float to the top. Stacia posts a new directive, "Starbucks." They drop a pin. "10 minutes. Contamination."

Will and Olivia start down the street, taking a left, and then a right, and then another left. They walk as quickly as they can until they see the Starbucks. It looks empty, yet they still head on over, walking into the store, spotting only two people in line. Nobody they recognize. Will and Olivia sit at one of the tables, watching for foot traffic.

"I'm here. Person in line coughing." It's another mod, Bert, detailing what sounds like a long line, someone falling over and seizing, coughing into the air. "Get here soon. Definite affliction."

Max chimes in: "Symptoms worse. Roanoke is for real. Take advantage. +100."

It results in a flurry of user responses:

"Here, advantage +50."

"Helping hand, +120."

"Status changing, confirmed, +75."

"Quarrel, potential fever. +15."

"Crowd, hysteria, play nice. +200."

"Cops, potential situation, advantage. +110."

Kaz makes an announcement and pins it to the top of #roanoke:

"Roanoke has proven its worth, affinites. Source confidants, be wary; authorities are enroute. Stacia on the move: Starbucks to nearby park to Max. Max has been admitted. Do not, I repeat do not, swarm the hospital. First 5 may accept visitation hours. Remainder, you lose points if you engage. Stay in sight, watch from afar. Seek out opportunities. Affliction is real. Roanoke will collapse within the hour. Get your exposure while you can. Again, any swarming or demonstrations of unmitigated advantage over the spurt and you'll be #silenced."

This must be a different Roanoke. Could it be that they were sent to the wrong Starbucks? The wrong city? Did Bert give them the wrong coordinates and details? There are plenty of questions, all of them having to do with the disconnect, how the Source provides a dizzying picture of a flash-outbreak, and yet here they are, two people sitting in an empty Starbucks, the hysteria they wanted completely denied.

Stunned, absolutely stunned.

Will doesn't know what to think.

It becomes altogether too obvious.

Olivia hyperventilates, the gravity of the situation hitting them both at the same time. They were abandoned, false information; the Source is somewhere else. It could be hazing, or really, it's what was always the case, they are untested and untrusted. The community doesn't know who they are, and unless they do something to prove themselves, they are decoys, people lesser than the whole. It makes the already wounded feel weaker, the lack of a crash causing both Will and Olivia to feel emptied out, such a hurtful thing, to be teased into traveling 8 hours to the wrong place, doomed to be a no-show, and worse of all, they will never know who is behind the spurt at Roanoke. The Source proves to be like so many other communities, insular and cliquish, built around favors rather than good faith. These people are better than you.

To think, though: How are they going to get back?

This is where she could say I told you so.

"Don't worry," Will says, off. "I have a plan B."

CHAPTER
VII

The thing about travel is that it's always easier to leave than to arrive. Will and Olivia have no leads and eventually do what needs to be done. They leave Roanoke empty handed and board another bus, their method identical the way home as it was the way there. This time, they sit together, daring to be spotted. At one point, Olivia rests her head on his shoulder. Will winces but gets used to it. He has no one else. There's nothing left to do.

Someone, kick them off the bus.

There's motive, two vagrants in broad daylight. Yet it's the 8-hour trek home, uneventful and normal. He exhibits no symptoms, and the Source proves that they are inadequate, just another affinite, yet unable to meet the baseline. This is what it must feel like to be lesser, a known inferiority. Will had all the potential to be a successful manager. Olivia had all the passion to become an artist and professor. It was the fact that they opened up to others, perhaps the wrong set of people, that ultimately scarred them so deeply, reshaped their psyches to the point of being unrecognizable. Nowadays, it's obvious: Nobody is looking for them.

There's still an apartment to come home to if home is the right word for it. Will expected the door to be kicked in, or at least unlocked. The traces of eviction, which was a long time coming, splayed all across the place. Instead, it's quiet, exactly as they left it. There's an odor in the air, which can be traced back to the bathroom, unflushed toilet, the excrement left having become liquefied over the last 48 hours, a dark brownish black sludge.

He flushes it and then looks at the faucet, doesn't wash his hands. What's the point?

Olivia goes to bed, stays in bed, has fallen into a deep depression since their abandonment. Will takes off his dirty clothes, stands naked in the mirror, examining his genitals for any indication, symptoms, a spot, anything.

A bust, he battles a panic attack and then takes a cold shower.

Toweling off, he goes into the other bedroom, stands at the foot of the bed, watching Olivia as she vacantly stares out the window.

"You okay?" he asks.

Olivia doesn't seem to hear him.

"I know," he says. "I'm sorry. I really believed them."

"I told you…" She lets out a sigh.

"What can I really say?"

He can't say anything. What's done is done. Of course, he told her about his plan B. What happened at the rest stop. There ought to be a conclusion to that encounter, a side effect, a symptom, something. Maybe it's because he can't stand the sight of her this way, or more so that he just wants to be in control, Will goes through with it. "I have a fever."

It gets her attention, Olivia looking up to see him there, naked.

"Really?"

He nods, tells her the same details again. He didn't use any protection, it was raw, and a foolish act if one wasn't seeking. Olivia sits up in bed, crawling forward to have a look. She inspects the area around the shaft, looking for blemishes, any sort of typical symptom, but because there isn't anything to be found, she lets go, staring at it with disgust, "Are you lying to me? You've lied to me before."

The way it's so easy for him to wear the lie, believing it like fact, it's almost obscene. A person shouldn't be so determined to hide in fabrication. He says it's true. A shrug, "It's early." They don't have a name for it yet, but he swears that it's there. He can feel the pathogen incubating, webbing with his cells. The symptoms will surface, he swears by it. It being nothing but intent. So when she goes in for another look, he adds some force. That's not usual for him, to break that sacred understanding for no physical contact. It comes as a surprise, seeing him get an erection so quickly, Olivia feeling it engorge while she grips hold of it.

"You want to feel light, right?" He moves in close enough that it has nowhere else to go but in her mouth.

She nods, lips wrapping around his shaft. It's her turn to have a taste.

"I freshly showered," he says, eyes closed. Clearly enjoying it. "It can taste unpleasant."

Olivia keeps going, minutes passing with nothing, until he makes a suggestion.

"Wait what?" Another surprise. Why now? So suddenly he sees her as a sexual object. The suddenness of the urge, like this is an imposter, not Will at all. He tells her to match him, take off the clothes. With enough persuasion, dangling the disease, she complies eventually. She takes it all off, and he takes control of the situation, lowering himself between her legs. His tongue centers on the clitoral hood while she squirms and fights back the feeling. This does not feel good, not to her. The whole thing is highly uncomfortable, and yet he goes down on her for an extended period of time, as if needing her to climax or the act was meaningless.

She will eventually, her entire body clenching, vaginal canal twitching, pushing out the gentlest brush of air, enough that he can feel it on his tongue. Afterwards, he slides into her while she's still dazed.

"Oh fuck," she shouts, the act completely unexpected.

"Just in case," he says, already going for it. He increases with each thrust. Olivia wraps the bedsheet around her arm, biting down on it, muffling every moan.

He recites the symptoms, "High fever, malaise, genital disfigurement, drippage, itchy and unpleasant rash…"

A moan. Perhaps she is beginning to enjoy the act?

He notices. She's getting wetter, making it more difficult for him to keep going without reaching climax.

So deep into the act, they might even consider what it looks like, their sex, to be watched. They are both young, malnourished enough that their skin is firm, her breasts perky, his penis circumcised, enough girth to cause a double take. He pulls out, needing a break, but she has gotten used to the sensation. It catches her off guard, and she says, "Put it back in."

He grips hold, feeling it pulsate. There's some ejaculate trickling out, he can see it dripping with a streak, dotting the bedsheets. She says it again, "Put it back in." A consolation, he turns her over, switching positions. Instinctively, she arches her back, ass in the air. He sees her asshole, beckoning for him to taste. And he does, pushing away all the usual thoughts, the caution of what might become of such an act. He uses the tip of his tongue to tickle the area, causing her to giggle and writhe. This goes on for a long time, enough that when he stops and slides back in, she has left a tiny streak of fluid where her vagina had been pressed against the mattress. Their bodies are dripping with sweat. Will talks about how it might come with a burning sensation, like their bodies will be on fire between their legs.

"Keep going," she says.

And he does. He fights the inevitable. Leaning in to kiss her, she pulls back.

"What are you doing?!"

He apologizes, "Sorry."

"Come on," she snaps. "On with it." The intent angers her, changing the dynamic. Olivia pulls on his pubic hair, "Give it to me."

It all goes deep into her, and never do they think about what this might become. She isn't on birth control. But it's all inside of her, and moments after release, they collapse onto the same urine soaked bed, struggling to catch their breath.

Like they were possessed, they fall back into their usual withdrawn selves.

"Did that just happen?"

"I think so."

They don't know what to talk about so they remain silent. There's a wave of shame that pulls them under, Will the first to fall asleep. Olivia hangs on a bit longer, fixated on all the new foreign feelings the act provided. Her mind drifts to a name, Charles, and her eyes go heavy at the thought of what Charles might provide. Will it be a fever first? She could almost climax a second time, the thought of what Charles will give her enough to orgasm.

She falls asleep before she can.

Will wakes up minutes later, needing to use the restroom. Afterwards, he struggles to fight back the paranoia, and once again gazes out the window for a long time. He suspects the landlord is nearby; he feels like he's being watched.

He checks the door, expecting to see someone, the landlord. Sees nothing. Looking at himself, he checks for any blemishes. Nothing.

Charles is a no show.

That day comes, a knock on the door, every paranoid urge validated. They're fighting over the fact that Charles yields nothing when they hear it, a fist clanging against the bulk of the door. Neither Will nor Olivia make any moves. Fear freezes them mid motion, the two of them standing in the kitchen, his face flushed red from anger, Olivia glistening from a fresh set of tears, when the door finally opens, a thin pale man wearing a beat up leather jacket and distressed black jeans, walks into the apartment and their lives mid-sentence.

"…Swear to god they are out to get me."

He slams the door shut, locks it and then joins them in the kitchen. Pushing past Will, he checks the cupboards, the fridge, looking for something to eat. "Damn, cleaned out. Got to keep up on this shit, man!" The man jabs him in the arm and then turns to Olivia, "You look well. I bet it's driving you crazy. It would drive me fucking crazy."

Taking off his jacket, hanging it on the back of a chair, he reveals a sweat-through band tee, both of his arms sleeved with faded tattoos. They've merged into one ongoing pattern, a dizzying display. He taps his forearm, "Got jabbed the other day. You can buy anything, you know? Just got to know where to look."

The guy leans against the counter, "Oh you know, it's this agency that moves from place to place. You can't find it because they don't stay much longer than a week. Swear to god, to get an invite, you basically need to be dying." He points at himself, "Yo. Dying. Terminal. It's liberating, actually. Don't need to feel pity for me. I'm alive right now. Who's to say anyone will be alive tomorrow? Anyway, I get this text message from a service I don't remember signing up for but I guess it's because I was hospitalized for a stroke a year back or so that I end up on their subscriber list or something. Oh man, let me tell you: A stroke really is a rush. It's scary because you don't know what's happening, and then you're deep in it and you have nothing else but to accept the fall. They're right when they say that your taste and smell go haywire. Then your left arm, a real struggle and a push, but you're not there for the actual stroke. You black out, feel me? And then you wake up and it's over, tubes injected into you. I had something strapped to me that helped me breathe. You're in that bright light, hospital experience. That part sucks but nurses come and feed you, check on you. It's kind of awesome actually. They pump you full of drugs, even if you tell them you want to feel it. I kept telling them I wanted to feel it. Every bit of it. I almost died, that kind of affliction is hard to come by. Everyone that averts death, hits rock bottom, they become better, more confident people. It's like they are Zen-like, monks because they've felt the full extent of human misery. I feel great," he winks at Olivia. "I feel the greatest I've ever felt and I'm terminal... yeah, yeah, so let nobody tell you you're less or something because they don't know shit until they've had a stroke, get terminal cancer, feel the full weight of a body, their body," he snaps his fingers, "becoming a foreign entity out to murder you. And fucking hell, let me tell you about the agency. That's what I was really getting at. Call it whatever you want but it's a shadow agency. They change everything every week but they peddle a good product. You can get jabbed with any strain you want. It'll cost, but they get it to you quickly and they manage to cut out the incubation period too. You feel the symptoms hours not days later. I got jabbed with this new sort of flu?" He taps his arm again, "Yeah, talk about fucking gnarly. It really hit hard. I was in bed, shivering for over a day. Zero appetite, completely out of my mind delirious from fever. It was awesome. I came out of that with such a high it was euphoric. Then it was over and the itch comes back, you know?" He looks at them both and then keeps talking, "Yeah, you both get it. Been a minute I see. That's what happens though, desperation kicks in and soon you're in a dumpster digging for anything. All you'll find there are the same strains and other bullshit. If you're like me, and I know you're like me, it's about finding the real shit. Man," he shakes his head, really exaggerating every motion, "I been around and back, even been part of a motherfucking online community of affinites, some dumb shit, right there. They say they are really for it when really they're mostly there for the power. They want all that power over others, validation, shit like that. I'm after the real shit. I want to feel it, every single thing. I want to know what death feels like long before it finally takes me. Motherfucker, I swear I want it to claim me. I want it to show me the full misery, and then I want to kick it and be like, I'm better off. Antibodies, may you build me a new fucking bridge, yo!" He laughs, looks over at Will and elbows him again, "Amiright?" The guy continues his frenetic diatribe, "They want all this power but I'm like, look at this agency, they got the power because they got people chasing after them. They have been made out to be an enemy, and because they're an enemy they're the ones with the real power. They get to make the next move. That's power. Me? I'm three moves ahead. I got the best they can give, and I already kicked it. It's done." He laughs, "There's this other world, man, like it's right there," he points at the floor. "It's here, invisible to our stupid fucking eyes, but it's here, and I've been telling everyone about it. All you got to do is look: There are deaths happening everywhere. Never mind the little deaths, fuck sex, all those STDs are for shit. Sex is 10 minutes of bodies fumbling for some meaning. Me, I've found the fucking meaning, just like I've found everything I need. I can die a happy fucking death. Kill me now if you want," he says, reaching into the right drawer, pulling out a knife. How did he know it was there? "Go right ahead, bleed me out. I probably got something you don't know. Oh man," he bares his teeth, "I definitely got something you don't. Don't you want it? Kill me, I dare you."

Will looks at the knife.

Olivia is trembling.

What just happened?

The guy bursts into laughter, "Woohoo! Ride that rush buddy," he says, taking the knife and cutting a few lines on his arm, "Easy. Fucking easy. I don't feel shit. But you…" He takes the knife to Will, cutting a thin red line on his palm, a morbid blood brothers act, "You feel it all."

Will grips his palm, blood dripping onto the floor, "What the…"

"Yeah you feel it all. We got to get you both some layers. And wouldn't you guess, I'm the guy to do it. Fuck those agencies, they sell stuff that's been stepped on. Me, I walk in that invisible world, finding realities in what people could only imagine while high out of their minds. There's so much out there to get us, it's kind of crazy to think that it hasn't already gotten everyone. Bro, people are dying, but so many are still alive. Worse, there's more of us every day. People grow up and fuck with this planet. It's a goddamn racket, and then if you dare at all to know someone, or be someone in public, they want something from you. Motherfucker, they feel like they are entitled to some part of you. It's bullshit and it's all a façade. Deep down, they're clamoring over what they want to see, not what they need to see. I see it, and then when they say, hey Zaff, that's not your real name. I'm like it's the name I respond to, real or not, so if you want to know me, even talk to me, you better get used to it. I'm Zaff, not Zeke. Zaff, not Ziff. Zaff. I'm Zaff."

The room falls silent, Zaff opening the floor for them to speak.

"You're Zaff," says Olivia.

He clicks his tongue, "But you knew that."

"Zaff, umm…" Will starts to say something but then stops.

Zaff waits patiently, until it's clear that they need more information. The confusion is trimmed away by acknowledging that they had been in Roanoke, they haven't been sick in a while, and they are, like Zaff, searching for something more to their existence. "You don't feel right, but you also don't know why you feel the way you feel." He shrugs, "Sound familiar?"

Olivia agrees, "You know us."

"I do," he says, waving the knife in the air. "Look at your cut." He's referring to Will's palm. When he checks it, much to his surprise, the cut has disappeared.

The response here is how, and this is the sort of thing that drives paranoia as much as passion. Something is amiss, this Zaff walks into their life with such ease as though they may have manifested him from thin air. The air itself, this concept of an unseen world, Zaff peddling something new, it's exciting if not also intimidating. They don't have a clue where this is going, or if this is even real, but when they see Will's palm healed, and when they realize Zaff knows their names, knows of his fraud and her miseries, Zaff quickly interjects himself into their chase, Will and Olivia unaware of where the next two months of their lives will take them.

"But you knew that," he says, like a refrain.

You knew before it happened, just like you'll see it coming long after there was any chance of preventing it from incubating.

Part Two

A BRAND NEW WORLD

CHAPTER

VIII

Zaff becomes the centerpiece of the final chapter in Will and Olivia's lives. Such a big personality, the mere thought that they might crash harder than ever before keeps all the curiosities at bay. For someone like Zaff, it's as much an opportunity as it is a form of escape. This is someone that has no friends, has seen the worst in people's lives, and perhaps inflicted a fair share of that hate and negativity onto others. Zaff is not his real name, and though what he says is true—he is dying—it isn't from what he says. This is no cancer, though he is indeed a Cancer, and in a way, a cancer on their lives. They just don't know it yet.

On this bright sunny desperate afternoon, they finally get what Will had feared all along. It starts with Zaff asking a question, "Have you ever had a fever of 103F or higher?"

"I've been delirious," Will says.

Olivia looks up from the laptop, "Yeah, I think so."

"You'd know if you broke that benchmark," Zaff says. "It's like I said, there's another world underneath all this." He paces around the apartment, sniffing the air, checking every corner, looking at the lived-in space with a unique set of eyes, a vision being revealed so effortlessly Will and Olivia, you could say, have become completely entranced by this guy's energy. He takes command of the moment, calling their attention to the topic at hand.

"After you hit 103, your mind expands and your vision blurs," he rests his hand on the TV. "Whatever seems normal takes on a different shape. I've gotten to the point where it almost scrambled my brain, my temperature was so high." He winks, "It rewires how you think. It makes you see past all this bullshit, the people, the money, the so-called American Dream... It shows you just how little we have control over anything."

They listen, watching as he turns on the TV, scrolling absent-mindedly through a streaming service. "None of this is real," he says. "It's all made to make us forget that we are real, our bodies are the source of everything. I don't find any of this entertaining, do you?"

Will shakes his head.

Olivia says, "Not really."

He laughs, "You both are funny. I like you." He looks back at the TV, "Both of you." Zaff scrolls through the documentary category, stops on one that focuses on the last pandemic, and then he says, "Sometimes that world I talk about so much, it pokes through and disrupts everything. We lived through it a little bit ago. Then things just went back to being the same. But really everybody was different. Most became more sensitive; others become more defensive. Me, I got the damn thing. Twice. It was fine, but nothing special. A little brain fog yeah, for a little bit, but even that went away. If only people did what I did and looked deeper."

Will doesn't seem to understand, "Look where?"

"Oh, you want a lecture, ha, I can give you a lecture," he grins, continuing to scroll through options. "In my experience, people don't like being lectured."

"I'm not people," says Olivia. "I want to know why we're so funny."

"Funny?" He stops scrolling. "Because you used to be like me."

"I'm nothing like you," Will says.

Olivia has a browser tab open, still watching the Source. They have moved on to another outbreak, somewhere in Orlando. There's the feeling of missing out, and then there's the feeling of having been abandoned, unwanted by an entire community of people.

This can't feel good, the fact that even after trying so much, neither Will nor Olivia feel any lighter, and the thought of crashing becomes less likely by the hour.

"Covid was a killer, but if you looked beneath the pandemic, you'll see that many of the medicines offered were even worse," Zaff advises. "You don't know what you have right there dripping from a faucet, maybe in your medicine cabinet."

"Okay," Will shrugs. "Show me."

There's no need to be kind here. It's about taking sides, this stranger talking the talk, they want him to prove it. It's how he is so willing to do so that gets them rapt, completely spun around his story. Zaff takes the TV and kicks it over, "Fine." The screen flickers twice and goes dead, "I'll fucking show you." Zaff turns his attention to the apartment. He returns to the kitchen, grabbing the knife, and proceeds to cut holes into the drywall. "I'll fucking show you." He tears into it, revealing insulation, plumes of dust and other debris going airborne. When he's done cutting a large hole in one of the common area walls, he turns to the carpet, the very same carpet that hasn't been cleaned the entire time Will has lived here. He pulls at its fibers, the blade used to uproot it from its fixture, peeling it back until it becomes easier, essentially rolling it off to one side. Underneath the carpet, the wood has become warped and discolored. "I'll show you." He turns to the pipes, loosening one until it begins leaking, the liquid itself isn't clean, a brownish tint. "I'm fucking showing you." Zaff goes into the bathroom, beckoning for them to follow. He digs through a toolbox under the sink, finding a wrench, and begins removing the toilet. "I'm showing you." The porcelain fixture begins to shake, the pressure of the water current causing a stir, when Will finally speaks up.

"Umm, hey," he says, half-heartedly. "This isn't your house."

"And it isn't yours," Zaff says, striking the pipe underneath the toilet. A low rumbling produces an undercurrent of sewage that leaks from the pipe and the base of the toilet. "Do you see now?"

There isn't a whole lot to see. Neither Will nor Olivia understand the context of all this carnage. Zaff tosses the entire apartment, and after he says, "You'd be surprised what you can find right here inside your house," he gets them both to take part. The bedroom is next. Zaff takes special interest in their mattress and their bedsheets. "Is that…?"

Olivia nods, "Urine."

Zaff shakes his head, "I'll show you."

It's all so confusing, the act, and yet why not? What have they got to lose? They are squatters, in essence, illegally staying in this apartment. Their stuff is no longer theirs; their lives no longer fully their own. Hmm, but they won't know that until much later, long after the bite.

He flips the mattress, takes the bedsheets and, after feeling the texture between his fingertips, he announces, "Potential." It's not over yet.

Will is told to "air out" the closet.

Olivia's tasked with laying out their dirty laundry.

The apartment turns into a cluttered mess.

"We devalue our sense of smell," he says. "Sight is often what we think of first when it comes to our senses. Then it's likely hearing. Then maybe taste. But smell? People be slacking on understanding what secrets lie within a single whiff." He sniffs the air, "Smell that?"

They do.

"You wouldn't be able to explain it, not in plain language, but what we're breathing in right now are all the dormant particles, including pathogens, that have been lying in wait among your clothes and your carpet, your walls and your plumbing. You both think too broadly; the world I see is revealed by smell. Our body odor for instance, I can tell that you've both washed recently, and what a waste because there's plenty living on these bodies of ours." He raises the knife, "You know, it could be as simple as a cut and an infection, and suddenly it's all revealed." He drops the knife, letting it fall to the floor, "Or it could be as simple as the right breath and in hours or days, you could be with something entirely new and novel."

"You're still not answering my question," Will says. "What the hell are you talking about?"

"I'm talking about power," he says. Letting it sink in, he breathes in deeply, "It's what you both call crashing. I see it for what it is. Power."

"Power…"

"It's what people want from you," he says. "It's what they are seeking when they hurt you, and when they threaten you. It's an act that has everything to do with making sure you never feel like yourself ever again."

"I won't let them," Olivia stammers. "Not anymore."

Zaff laughs, "And that's why you both are so funny. You still think it's an option."

"It is an option," Will says. "We don't have to do anything we don't want to do."

"That's where you're wrong," Zaff grins. "Me, I'm in control of my senses; I can see it all, but it came at a price." He coughs, spitting up blood. "No regrets."

"How much longer do you have?" Will says.

"Not long," Zaff shrugs. "Maybe long enough. Not really sure."

Olivia clenches one of the bedsheets, "You're terminal."

"You say it like that's a bad thing," Zaff wipes his bloodied hand across his pant leg. "What you think is bad could be the best thing that's ever happened to you." He looks around the room, "I think they'd agree."

Before it can be asked (who are "they"?) Zaff falls to one knee, clenching his right side. Breathing heavily, he spits another dark blotch onto the floor, Olivia gazing at it with interest. Will walks over to help him to his feet, but Zaff waves him off, "They want me to feel this, and I have no other reason but to let them," he winces. "But fuck, it's getting so much worse."

"What are your symptoms?" Will has an inherent need to know. Zaff is battling something he's never seen before. If he gets close enough, maybe he'll contract it too.

"Fever, muscle spasms, internal hemorrhaging…" Zaff trails off, another dire spell of pain coursing through his organs. "The usual." Zaff has another task, "Medicine."

"Medicine," Olivia says, disappointed. Shouldn't he fully enjoy every symptom?

"Give me medicine!" Zaff raises his voice, a first. They haven't seen him frazzled, much less on the brink of anger. The bigness of his personality and the relative cool factor to his intended persona disappear as he battles a wave of full-bodied tremors.

"Painkillers?" Will hesitates, "Painkillers, right?"

"Medicine," Zaff hisses, jaw clenched. "Bring all medicine."

Will retrieves the medicine, returning with dozens of bottles, various painkillers and antibiotics. "Here, umm, which-what do you need?"

But maybe it's too late. Zaff has collapsed to the floor, unconscious. Olivia watches it happen in complete disbelief and more than a little jealousy.

"What happened?" Will asks.

She gives him a look, "I want what he's having."

Zaff is carried over to the couch, where he sleeps off an attack. Will and Olivia remain in the bedroom, door locked, a private conversation believed to be entirely theirs, and nobody else's to partake. Will talks about the tremors, "I can't make any sense of it."

Olivia agrees, "He says he's dying. I want to know what he's dying from."

"Maybe he doesn't know," Will says.

"He knows," Olivia rolls her eyes. "Guy goes on and on about some other universe or something, and then he tosses your apartment saying that we could find anything we want right here, but as far as I can tell, I feel the same."

"I'm losing it," Will nods.

"Look," she raises her hand. "I'm shaking like having a withdrawal."

"I'm sorry," Will confesses the thing about his plan B. "Something came over me."

She sighs, "I would say I'm surprised but nothing surprises me anymore." She frowns, "You're no different."

"I know," he says.

"I'd leave but this is the best I got," she explains. "Moment I find a way out, I'm cutting you out."

"Same," Will agrees. "But what is it about this world, the thing he's talking about?"

"I guess we'll find out," Olivia shrugs. "He does look a little sickly."

"Those tattoos," Will shivers. "It's like they were melted on."

"I know," Olivia says, her eyes wide. "I wonder how he did it."

There's a lot to learn, and much more to dredge up from Zaff's downward spiral. Their private conversation may not be so private, yet in this moment, they speak with such candidness, explaining to each other that it's a transaction. Everything they will ever do to and with each other is a transaction, and this Zaff, he walks into their lives like how they walked into their own, with a sense of disrespect and disregard to legitimize the next foray into self-destruction.

At the end of any given day, who really gives a shit?

Every accident that evoked another notch to the prevailing sinking feeling that makes Will paranoid and Olivia forever troubled by her own body, it all ends up the same: with an accident and another moment of acknowledgement that maybe they were not brought into this life, and onto this earth, with the best of intentions.

Zaff comes to laughing, calling the attack "a memorable one." He goes on to explain what happened, "I've been getting these, and it's simple stuff at first, a little eye twitch or maybe a jolt, like a muscle clenches on its own… but then it starts to fuck with my vision and my hearing, and then I start getting dizzy. Turns out that's all part of the body breaking down, and all that coughing up blood? I've had that for years. Relic from a previous encounter. It's not all that bad, actually," he laughs. "It gets a good reaction. This thing I've got now, the attacks send me into such an intense burst of pain, I always black out and have very vivid dreams. They are full of colors and oddities, teeth loosening and falling out, running from something, it's always something different. I wake up from them feeling immortal, just absolutely incredible." Zaff flexes his biceps, "It's incredible!"

"This world," Olivia changes the subject. "Where is it?"

Gesturing to the tossed apartment, "Oh, sorry, I may have been delusional but that's because this attack was mounting. This, this is what I meant. There's a whole world of destruction, and behind that underbelly, we have so many opportunities to feel pain, to contract a new strain." Zaff grins, "I started almost a decade ago, and the things I have inflicted, and the things I have felt, oh man, you both wouldn't be so funny if you saw even a flicker of what I've done to people, to this fucking world. This piece of mother-fucking-shit world!" There's that same larger-than-life persona from before, poking through the remnants of the latest attack, "If you knew, you'd be laughing right with me, because motherfucker you better goddamn believe that this is the tip. The fucking tip! I tossed the apartment because I could. I cut you and healed you, Will, as a tease, to make a fucking point. Only reason I stopped by to see you both was because I knew another attack would happen, and it's better to inflict some of it on others, scare them maybe, at least get a laugh out of it."

The look on Will's face, it's exactly Zaff's desired effect.

He laughs, "That's it right there."

To Olivia, he says, "You got more guts than this coward. But hey, that's also why I'm not just going to walk back out. I got it, you know. The thing you want..." That thing they want... it's what Zaff already has. "All you got to do is ask."

Olivia takes the initiative, "I want it."

"Good," Zaff says. "I'll show you."

"How do you know so much?" Will asks, mystified by the turn of events.

"I don't know shit," Zaff says. "I just act like I do. Power. Again it's about power. Now how about a glass of water?"

Zaff waits until Will isn't looking to bite down, teeth sinking deep into his flesh.

"I said I'd show you," he grins, Will's blood on his bottom lip. "So there it is. It's done. No going back now."

"Fuck," Will winces. It's a deep gash, teeth marks in a perfect U-shape across his bicep.

"They can't take me yet," Zaff says, "but I can take you for a spin."

"That really hurt," Will says, watching blood pool where Zaff's molars pierced his skin.

"Now bite her," Zaff says, a new task.

"Huh?"

"You heard what I said," Zaff says, sitting up. "Go over to Olivia and bite her the way I just bit you."

There's really nothing Will can do, not anymore. The moment for a savior has passed, leaving behind only creatures of a palpable darkness, people like Will and Olivia that dwell in the destruction that take from them any possibility of being able to enjoy the moment, any chance of ever being able to achieve a sense of happiness. In its place, there is purity only in the destruction, the act of inflicted pain, and most of all, in the crash. Will has no choice but to dig his teeth into her warm flesh, like a vampire, and really they are vampires of a lesser breed, seeking every strain that will threaten to finally take their lives. The cowards of the world can't handle death on its own; they need to suffer before they can finally reach their last breath. So Will and Olivia will suffer. Zaff will be their savior figure, a person only from a glance. If they looked past all that they want from him, they'd see more than a criminal and a troubled being. They'd see that Zaff exists for vampires just like them, to ensure that they will remain cowardly and cruel in all that they will do amid their first and final downward spiral.

Will bites down on her forearm, Olivia watching in amazement.

Perhaps surprising isn't how she takes it in stride, not even a single note of pain, only pleasure, on the verge of excitement, rather it's how Olivia sucks on his wound, licking it repeatedly, forcing him to do the same. A little creativity, after all, goes a long way. Zaff seems to enjoy the sight, seated on the couch, his elbows on his knees. He's found two new specimens to exploit, and what happens during their time together, it's the stuff nobody ever wants to talk about. The destruction they leave behind remains invisible because people don't like seeing their brand of carnage. It happens most often behind closed doors, internally, the body the real warzone. Their bites will heal over and become barely a scar before anything happens. Along the way, though, Zaff will enjoy his final days, and these hopeless souls, they'll never again have a clear thought. Every living moment will be disturbed, bled through with the terrors they inflict and endure.

CHAPTER

IX

They pick out a car from the apartment parking lot. Any will do, but Zaff is dying, a ticking clock, so they go for the Corvette. Why the hell not? They were going to steal a car anyway. Neither Will nor Olivia makes a move for the driver's seat, which might be all the evidence one needs to fully frame this threesome, the dynamic of their situation. Zaff gives Will a look that says it all, Don't want to drive? Will shakes his head, looks a little intimidated.

"I'm afraid of driving," he says.

Zaff laughs, looks over at Olivia.

"Never learned how to drive," she shrugs. She decides to ride shotgun, Will forced to slide into the backseat.

"You both are so goddamn funny," Zaff shakes his head. "For real, a laugh riot."

It's how Zaff doesn't need to hotwire the sportscar, by touch alone able to fire up the engine, pulling out of the parking space, pointing them in a direction that makes it clear that they'll never see that apartment again.

"I'm going to show you a brand new world," he says, pushing down on the gas.

He reaches 80MPH, dodging traffic, and there's never a moment when being pulled over is even a possibility.

Who is scared right now? Will grips onto the car seat, grit teeth, eyes glued to the road ahead. Olivia enjoys the air, breathing in as much of it as she can, Zaff noting that you never know what might be riding the air.

"It's kind of scary," she says.

"What is?" Zaff says, switching lanes.

"Meeting people," she says, stealing a glance at the vehicle in the next lane. "Nobody is ever who they say they are."

"I agree," says Zaff. "Having a body is a prison, doing time until the walls wrinkle, the ceiling collapses in on itself, succumbing to the strain of so much struggle."

"Poetic," she says.

"I'm a poet," Zaff says.

"Are you published?" Will chimes in from the backseat.

It's like Zaff doesn't hear him, changing the subject, "This new world, it'll be full of people. But it's okay, because you're going to have armor." He cracks his knuckles, "You're going to be like me, impenetrable in the face of all that judgment."

They make it to the highway, and it's around this time that Will asks a logical question, "Where are we going?"

Zaff looks at him in the rearview mirror, switches lanes. He's got them right where he wants them. Bitten and suddenly bold, two young chasers that'll soon discover that Zaff needs them just as much as they need him.

They're driving for about an hour when Zaff takes an exit. "I want you to see something," he says, narrowly avoiding a pedestrian. "You take your life in your hands," he shouts, slamming his fist against the ceiling of the Corvette.

"Just so you know," he says. "I won't always be here."

"I'm not so sure you're here right now," Will says.

"That's a good guy," Zaff grins. "Everyone out to get you."

They are no different. Neither will ever forget the conversation they had, their friendship really being one of opportunity and chance. Olivia has no other recourse. Will is doomed to the shadows of society. Zaff is terminal, perhaps the recipient of many names, a path of destruction that he will reveal to them, piece by piece. Firstly, they end up at his childhood arcade, which has now grown in size to become one of the largest in the country.

He slams on the brakes, "Come on, out, out!"

They're filed into the arcade, Zaff greeting the person at the front register, "Howdy. Damn this place is loud!"

They are paid to be friendly, to admit everyone willing to play.

"$25 for entry? What a steal."

"Thanks, yeah, we've got hundreds of games. All on free play. You'll see that there's a little bit for everyone."

Zaff raises his hand, "Say no more. And hey, I got this." He pays for their entry and then he escorts them down one of the aisles.

"People escaping reality," he says. "It's hilarious to me. I have been here so many times but never have I been since I've seen the world from a different perspective."

Will stops at one machine, recognizing the game, "I used to play this all the time."

"Oh really?!" Zaff approaches the machine, giving it an in-depth look. He taps one of the buttons once, a second time. Wrapping his hand around the joystick, he looks at them and asks, "How many people do you think have played this game?"

"Thousands, easy," says Olivia, who looks down the aisle, perhaps seeing a machine from her past.

"How many hands on this stick, how many fingers pressed these buttons…" Zaff presses start, the game coming to life. "How many times have people failed, how many times have people beaten this game."

"I don't know," says Will.

A flick of the wrist, a single glance at the game screen, and

Zaff shows them a bit of that world, the one where everything is predictable, people are an obvious danger, and the games they play are as mechanical as this arcade game.

"Hey, I was playing that." It's a voice from another time, or really, it's a voice of a man that decides to target Zaff. "Hey you."

Zaff keeps playing.

Will looks at the man. He's got some bulk to him. Must work out.

"You hear me, huh?" The guy takes another step. "I was playing that. I just had to use the bathroom but I'm back now." The guy doesn't get a response. He looks at the screen and watches Zaff fumble a jump and instantly, the guy judges him, his entire worth, all because of one mistake in a game built purely on fantasy. "Leave it to the pros."

"You hear something?" Zaff looks at Will, "I think I hear a ringing in my ears."

Will clears his throat, still too afraid of the repercussions, not yet seeing what Zaff sees. He's in the moment, rather than seeing three moves ahead. This is the part where that world Zaff's talking about shows itself. The guy tries something, laying a hand on Zaff, only for it to end up in Zaff's grip, his fingers beginning to bend back, far enough that the guy should feel something. They're all watching it unfold like it's fresh out of a video game. Fingers freshly broken, the guy isn't screaming, no pain registered. Zaff holds off on the effect, wanting it to be so decimating, an all-at-once realization that this guy has messed with the wrong person, and in doing so, he will never again be the same. One person can ruin your life.

He takes the guy's broken hand and wraps it around the joystick, "I'll leave it to the pros." Zaff takes a step back from the machine, gesturing for Will and Olivia to follow him down another aisle. When they are out of sight, they hear it. The guy wailing in pain, followed by a crescendo of voices, everyone wanting to know what happened.

No one will trace it back to them, Zaff already moving forward, taking their place at another machine, this one with two brightly colored guns, a shooter. Zaff takes the player one gun and points it directly at Will, "You want to die?"

Speechless, Will shakes his head, "No."

"What about you?" This time it's Olivia who says, "Yeah."

"Fair enough," Zaff shrugs, aiming at her foot. He pulls the trigger.

Olivia collapses to the floor, the sound of a gunshot echoing throughout the arcade. People scatter, Olivia bleeds onto the floor. Zaff laughs, "You're all so funny."

See how it can change so suddenly? Zaff blinks and the bullet never happened. It's there and then it's not. However, he doesn't acknowledge her temporary pain, instead lifting it and removing all but the lesson in need of being learned.

"If there's even a possibility of danger, people won't stand up for you. They only think of themselves." They watch as someone runs past, pushing Will out of the way. "They get hysterical, everyone thinking as one shameless unit." Zaff frowns, "But all they're doing is putting themselves into even more danger." Outside someone trips and falls into the street. A car follows shortly behind, there to collide, a visible crash that leaves someone crippled. It happens for effect, to make a point, but as Zaff sighs, the person stands up, stunned and confused. Like nothing ever happened.

"What... the fuck?" Will says, watching in disbelief.

"Ever had a temperature of 103F or higher?" He brings it back up. "When you do, everything changes. It's a brand new world."

Blood trickles down the corner of his mouth.

The arcade returns to normal. It's an illusion for nobody but them; Will and Olivia go back to trying out different games. Zaff hides in the bathroom, the full extent of the attack beginning to take hold. He sits on the toilet seat, wiping blood from his mouth. With every wince, his body conjures an untold onslaught of pain.

No doubt about it, the symptoms are getting worse. His vendetta of destruction just might have an end date sooner than expected. Zaff looks at his reflection, his skin glistening from sweat. This will really take it out of him. He won't be well for a long time. Zaff doesn't want them to see this, not the full extent, at least not yet. With all the blood comes blindness, the pain causing him to fall to the dirty tile floor, blacking out for a half hour. In the cushion of the nightmare unfolding, he flees into the future, what will become of this arcade. It had been a place of purity and nostalgia. The arcade is a net positive, something that conjures happiness, a bright spot on this planet. All the more reason for someone like Zaff to inflict the same degree of pain he is dealt onto the aisles and audience, destroying any possibility for the arcade to feel anything but oppressive, a place marked (and therefore tainted) by tragedy.

Yeah, that's how it'll play out.

Like a game.

Will and Olivia are swept up by the sounds of the arcade, momentarily lost in their own game-runs. There might even be a genuine laugh, a smile out of Olivia's mouth as she shoots her way through a zombie horde. Will is focused on a fighting game, loving the way each button press results in another strategic play. There's no pressure, no element of humanity judging their performance. They seemingly leave their bodies, becoming protected and contained in a world of nostalgia. The world they'll know, it'll come knocking just as soon as Zaff rises to his feet.

For now, a temporary reprieve, an interlude that makes it seem like there's a chance.

Everything will be okay.

He comes to, dry blood caked to his mouth and eyelids. Zaff yawns, feeling once again invincible, the fresh absence of pain brings with it ideas. Lots of ideas. Inspired by a nightmare gifted to him by his affliction, as though the virus tells (and controls) the host, Zaff washes his face clean, the water turning a dark pink, and then he grins at himself in the mirror. He strikes the glass, shattering it with his fist. He bleeds from fresh cuts, but then wipes his hand against his pant leg, the cuts instantly healed. He swipes a large glass shard. It'll come to good use.

Out of the bathroom, he saunters up and down the aisles, looking for the first body in need of some trimming. Spotting a man with a baseball cap playing a racing game, Zaff grabs a stool and sits down next to the guy.

"How's it going?"

Baseball cap doesn't look away from his gameplay, "Umm what?"

"Third place," Zaff eyes the screen. "You're going to have to do better than that. In this world, there is only first place and a fuck ton of losers. You're not a loser are you? Bro, like I can tell just by the way you're cutting corners that you're going to lose. That's no good! Life's a game, man, and you're really blowing it."

"Man, fuck off!" Baseball cap miscalculates the turn and his digital car slams against the side of the track.

"You already lost," Zaff says, leading with the glass shard. It would be too easy and obvious to cut along the man's neck, so Zaff instead goes for the eyes. He pins baseball cap against the plastic cockpit and cuts off the man's eyelids. Zaff is still getting over the attack, so his hearing is a little sensitive, so the man, though screaming loudly, has his voice muted. "What a shame. Don't get in the driver's seat if you aren't willing to do anything to 'win.'"

He leaves baseball cap passed out at the machine and starts up another aisle. No one sees him coming, because that's how he imagines it. Poor teenager playing Mortal Kombat and doing a good job of winning against the competition. Poor man playing a shoot 'em up, filming his run, an indication that he is aiming for greatness. Poor display of people minding their own business, right as Zaff does the following in quick succession.

He antes up, challenging the teenager in the fighting game. They go best two out of three, and because Zaff has another game in mind, he lets the kid win. At the moment of declaring, Finish Him! Zaff complies, slamming the kid's forehead against the control deck, the left joystick shoved down the teenager's throat as he gags, dizzy enough for the final few strokes. Zaff thrusts the kid's face through the screen with a tremendous and perhaps impossible amount of force, the electric current taking the kid's pulse, body limp and occasionally twitching.

"Fatality," Zaff announces, surging with power.

Zaff takes the man's camera and spoils both the game run and footage, "You see, this guy's very serious. He really wants a top score. How many hours does a person put into something before they become a master? Years? Probably. It takes a lot of practice. It looks like he's having a good run, though. The score, look at that score!" Zaff watches as the man's ship flies into a wave of gunfire, blowing up. It's too surprising and unexpected a move, the man remains on his stool, unable to react, leaving Zaff to film the entirety of his lecture and subsequent strangulation.

He leaves behind dying bodies, the destruction is pure evil, not that anyone will notice. At another cabinet, Zaff watches from down the aisle as a middle-aged woman enjoys playing an old favorite. It's a game from her past, a game that hearkens back to a simpler time. Zaff can see the wholesomeness of this scene, and allows for some space, for it to exist longer than most before he takes it away. There is no "letting it pass." He'll take her hand, and lead her to her demise. They'll walk over to the front of the arcade, leaving it for the alley out back. Zaff makes it up as it goes, but sees that she's ready. There's no fun in that. She needs to beg for her life. Zaff pulls the air from her lungs, then lets her breathe. Violently coughing, the woman is tortured until Zaff recognizes just how cruel this is and perhaps it comes back, a glimmer of the person he was, so long ago, because he demonstrates mercy. He cuts along her throat, ending the torture.

Gone as soon as it arrived, Zaff is back in character, making his way back into the arcade.

Will.

Olivia.

He'll be with you soon.

"Come, you don't want to miss this." Will and Olivia join Zaff at the front desk of the arcade. Zaff strikes up a conversation with the employee at the register, "I'm having just the greatest time! So many games, so much history! It's wild!"

"Thank you," the employee says. "We're proud of being such a good thing to so many people."

"This place is one of a kind," says Zaff.

"What do you guys think?"

"It's great," Olivia says.

"I agree," Will grins. "I've never seen so many games before."

"Yeah, yeah," Zaff nods. "Oh right. So there's one game…" He reveals a blue light gun, removed from its source. "The machine kind of crapped out. See? The gun just came right off."

The employee apologizes, "These machines do take a beating. May I ask which machine it was?"

"I don't remember the name," Zaff says, placing the gun on the glass counter. "But I can show you," he gestures down one of the aisles.

"Absolutely," says the employee, leaving his post. It's exactly what Zaff wanted, to get the guy away from the counter, in plain view. He strikes the employee in the stomach, a gut punch, causing him to fall to the floor. Zaff places a knee against the employee's throat.

He tells them, "He's sick."

The employee tries to say something.

"I'm showing you, really showing you," he winks. "He's sick and you'll want what he's got. It'll be a nice one to keep you occupied."

Will gazes down at the poor employee, "The name?"

"My name…" The employee struggles to break free, Zaff adding additional pressure. "No, the name. You could be anyone. It doesn't matter."

It seems Zaff already knows, "It's Nick. You'll feel it in your stomach, pure violence for 24 hours."

"What's the catch?" Olivia asks.

Zaff raises his eyebrow, "Who says there's a catch?"

Olivia sighs, "Please."

Will repeats Zaff's words, "You could be anyone. It doesn't matter."

"You both matter," Zaff says. "I wouldn't be here, showing you, if you weren't capable of so very much."

They stand their ground, employee kicking and choking. Zaff presents them with a choice. Snap of a finger, he can make it all go away. It's up to Will and Olivia.

Does the employee live or die? Light gun or a different method?

The deaths littering the arcade floor, do they stick or do they fade away, removed to inevitably give others another day? One thing's for sure, it'll be a tough choice to make.

The destruction of the arcade, they may not have been privy, but Zaff chooses to make them complicit. The decision is theirs, a choice that has everything to do with Zaff maintaining control of them and the situation.

CHAPTER

X

"What's it going to be, then?" The pure pleasure is painted across the aisles. Zaff's vindictive destruction of the arcade, it may feel currently like the end of an era, but it can all disappear.

They just need to say the words.

Everything could so easily fade, a stain on this earth made temporary, but perhaps it's more like they don't yet understand what's at stake.

Will takes the light gun in his hands.

Zaff likes what he sees, grinning widely, "What's on your mind, Will?"

Olivia takes a step closer, reaching for Will's free arm, "Don't do it."

All the more reason for him to go through with it. Will raises the gun, aiming down the sights. There's only one real target. He aims right between the eyeballs and pulls the trigger. Click. Another pull of the trigger, the plastic gun does as it was made, a little fake recoil, but otherwise a simple and would-be satisfying click.

"You could have just said yes," Zaff winks, letting the employee go.

In fact, there's more than just the one to let free, the entirely of all that painted pleasure, blood red stains against an aural soundscape of would-be bliss, it unravels between Zaff's fingertips, and there's only Will and Olivia to know what might have occurred.

It was made in nobody's image.

Zaff gave them the choice and it was a decision forged by inaction, so the arcade will live another day. It will spread cheer to people that might never see the world unfolding between blinks, the world dealt as brand new, full of untold terrors, and the brink of people willing to lay claim to all that could be yours.

There's nothing left for them here. Zaff has made his point. They return to the Corvette, only this time it's a blue sedan, nothing special. "Where did…" Olivia starts to ask, and then stops.

"Now you're starting to get it," Zaff says, before coughing and spitting blood. "Don't worry," he raises his hands. "I'll drive."

This moment acts as a pivot. Zaff entered their life as a mentor figure, only to become a menace. Here, post-arcade, he becomes more of a colleague. In time, he will become a victim. By then he'll be down to a few final breaths, and both Will and Olivia will have also pivoted on their descent to rock bottom.

Time for a little show and tell. "I showed you something from my past," Zaff says. "Now you show me something of yours."

Olivia in the front passenger seat, she squirms at the thought of what Zaff might ask of her. When history tells her that it's a transaction, almost always take and no give, the body and eventually more to draw from the mind, she is quick to take a stance. This was the reason she turned to chasing the crash, the feeling of lightness that keeps all this anxiety from ever reaching her reality. Zaff calls attention to her panicked breaths, "You've got plenty of time."

The tell—Will refusing to make eye contact.

The solution—Zaff speaks directly to his past, right on down to cadence and tone, "…and to think the CFO believed that guy. It was an opportunity and equally a choice made by both you and him.

He seemed so trustworthy at first, this guy with about as much, or as little, to lose as you. Chase reveals one side of the security flaw. Only thing you really did was connect the dots. It's the fact that you aren't behind bars right now that says it all: Chase made money off the knowledge, and the company that gave you life, all it did was…"

"Take it away," Will says. "I don't know where he lives anymore."

Zaff turns the ignition, sedan coming to life, music blaring out of every speaker. He turns the volume down low enough, "It's true. He moved." Before Will can ask any questions, Zaff turns up the volume and pushes the sedan to the limit, another speed demon spectacle. They're heading into Will's past.

"Why'd you do it?" Zaff asks.

Olivia flashes a look of concern, "Maybe he didn't have a choice…"

"He has a reason, and there's always a choice," Zaff says. "I'm just curious. This is the kind of thing that keeps a person from moving on."

"Looking back at it, I think I liked how it made me feel," says Will.

Zaff nods, a clear understanding can be traced across planning and intent.

"Chase being there just made it easier to keep going when I had my doubts."

"And it wasn't even about the money," Zaff says, making an assumption.

"Nope, it wasn't."

Zaff slams on the brakes, a red light. Why stop now? He runs every red light. The reason for stopping now has everything to do with Will and Olivia and nothing to do with Zaff. On the crux of that pivot of roles, Zaff is a mere driver. Though there are suspicions, and it would be foolish to think of someone like Zaff of lacking an agenda; however, on this drive through tragedy lane, Zaff gives away control, piece by piece, until it becomes clear to both people in his presence that they are here not because he needs friends. No. They are here to be his confidants.

"Power," Will admits. "It was about power."

There's an echo, a refrain repeated across every block, on the other side of every hurdle. The power builds itself into something so much bigger. Everything's real, and because it is real, anything can change. "You just have to want it," says Zaff. "Manifest their misery."

Will begins to get restless, and it's because of this that the days-long drive passes in a single blink. Another test, perhaps. Zaff seeing if either needs to find logic or reason in this world, or if his own body once again showing signs, blood tearing out of both his eyes, is enough for Will and Olivia to understand. And they do. Even if they are not yet willing to accept. The car is parked in the driveway of a two-story home, pretty nice, well-kept lawn and a nice fresh coat of paint. The house is fairly new; the owner's even newer to the neighborhood. Zaff remains in the driver's seat, "Go on ahead." He looks in the glove compartment and finds some tissues. "I'll catch up." He cries blood, the waves of pain will be next. Zaff would rather that they don't see him this way—no, not because it makes a person vulnerable; he's long past any feelings of vulnerability—rather, it's something they will have to experience for themselves. Kind of like dodging spoilers, why ruin some of the crash?

"Umm…" Olivia watches the blood trickle down his face.

"Quickly," Zaff waves. "He's waiting for you at the door."

There they are, Will and Olivia, chasers unknowingly being chased, knocking on the door of the man that threw Will under the bus. Nobody answers the door anymore, but they will if you keep knocking on the door. One set of fists becomes a second, Olivia approaching the door with the same patter, an onslaught of increasing aggression until there he is, a man named Chase.

The look on his face says it all: How did you find me?

No greetings or helloes. This is all about goodbyes.

Will pushes past him, entering the foyer. Olivia follows, looking back at the sedan, just in time to see Zaff seizing, a full-bodied attack. It's happening. It's been happening more often. Eventually, there will be a day when the attack persists, leaving Zaff a body coming apart at every joint. For now though, he suffers the attack, giving way to a glimmer of a shot at vengeance. And there will indeed be vengeance. Will looks around the foyer, "It's been a minute." He gives Chase the once-over, "You look good."

"And you look like shit," Chase frowns. "What the hell are you doing here?"

Olivia speaks up, "We're going to fuck you up."

It's really that simple. Gets the mind working. Be honest. Be up front. They are going to indeed fuck Chase up. The possibilities are endless, it seems. Firstly, there's a need. Afterwards, there'll be a want. Will already has need filled out; this man ruined his life.

So say it.

"You ruined my life," Will says. Taking a look around at the place, it looks like he's been living the big life. "How big is that TV?"

Chase isn't playing along, taking a full step back, arms crossed, "You need to get the fuck out right now. Before I call the cops."

"Ah boo," Olivia makes a face. "Don't be boring."

"What's the point if you can't mess with people?" Will answers the question, "You messed with me, probably even had it planned from the start, didn't you?"

Olivia walks into the next room, "He did."

"Yeah, I think you really did," Will steps forward, trying confrontation on for size. "You knew it all along. Thought you could get away with some of the cash."

"The TV is at least 80 inches," Olivia says.

"That TV was bought using money that sprouted from my demise," Will says. Right in his face, he whispers, "I'm back from the dead."

If this comes off as a derivative of an action flick, something lifted from the tropes, a formulaic act, it's because it is. Zaff suffers in the driver's seat, the tremors sending his head into the center of the wheel. They can hear the car horn from outside, acting as embellishment for Will's suddenly confident character shift. Zaff suffers the attack, giving Will the confidence to make the jump, let it all fall into place, so that he may begin his latest and greatest crash. What better way to get it started than with confronting the demon of his past?

"This is stupid," Chase sighs, turning to walk down the hall. "I'm calling the cops."

Olivia bursts into action, screeching as she jumps onto Chase's back, the full weight and scale of impact causing him to crash against the hardwood floor. His shoulder absorbs most of the fall. Olivia scratches him across the face, Will tapping her on the shoulder.

"It's okay. Let him up."

She licks the sweat off Chase's forehead and laughs.

Will waits until he starts to climb up before he lands a kick, forceful enough to send Chase back to the floor. "Whoops. It slipped."

A second attempt leads to another kick, this one hitting Chase across the face. That starts the water works, his nose flowing blood.

"Looks like you broke it," Olivia says, examining every action like a scientist.

He keeps going, "You thought you could use me and then lose me. And for a while, I believed it. I believed that my life was over. For a long time, it seemed like it was. I lost everything." Remembering Olivia, he flashes her a sinister grin. "Then something happens, maybe you meet someone, and things change. Even the end passes on to a new beginning. I'm looking at… a brand new world." Taking words right out of Zaff's latest lecture, Will surges with confidence. Riding high, feeling impenetrable, Will has the entirety of the scene unfolding in his fingertips. All he needs to do is act. This is where

Olivia loses interest, walking into another room, understanding that Will needs time alone with his past. He needs time to inflict a brand new world of harm and heartache.

Where to start?

"Your wife will be home soon," Will says. How does he know this?

It's what anybody would be thinking, and it's because of the pain outside that something else can be manifested. It's up to Will to ensure that the want cultivates from a caustic source. That source will soon walk through that front door, joining Will in his inaugural moment.

"She won't be seeing you, though." Will laughs. "It's a bummer. Really, it is. How foolish to think that you could do such wrong and think you won't be punished." He gets down on all fours and shouts in Chase's face, "You are going to be punished! I want you to know what you've done to me! You made it so that I can never work again. I lost everything—my girlfriend, my savings, my sanity! When you went and pointed blame square on me, you immediately made it so that I was banished to the margins of society. I've dug through dumpsters. I've had dozens of diseases. I have licked semen clean off a stranger's dick. I've done it all and was sober, completely lucid doing so. And what did I get? Strength. I got strength. With every new low, I gained knowledge that I could only go up from there. Higher. I went from nothing and total loss to finding someone, and feeling something. I let go of all that loss and look who I found?"

Zaff times it perfectly, walking inside. Mere sight of him sends Chase into terror, visibly shaking. Begging Will to stop. "Please no."

"I've heard that before," Zaff says. He pushes Chase over, laying him on his back, and then straddles him, "So this is the guy."

"How did I know that his wife's gonna be home in 25 minutes?" Will asks, barely a whisper, but then it becomes clear that not all questions need answers and he pushes on, provoking the decimating fear in his former partner and "friend."

"There are no friends," Will says, "They're just people that want something from you."

Zaff grins, full agreement, "We're friends."

Will looks at him, "Yeah, yeah we're friends."

Zaff pulls a switchblade from a pocket and says, "Can I be your friend?" He uses the sharp blade to cut Chase's shirt, peeling it off until he's fully bare chested. Zaff plays with his chest hair, curling the coarse black hair around his fingers. "So, friend, what you want to do first?"

From another room, they can hear Olivia shout, "Cut his penis off!"

Zaff shrugs, "Anything goes."

"May I?" Will wants to switch places.

"What confidence." Zaff winks. "I love it."

Handing over the switchblade, Will takes the blade, cutting himself across the cheek, making sure to draw blood and for those body fluids to remain on the blade. The blade is forced into Chase's mouth. "Close. Shut it. There's a good boy." The blade in his mouth, Will keeps a hold of it while discussing old times. "Remember when we met the first time in person? It was like we had known each other for ages. We chatted about movies and chatted about growing up thinking money was magic. Then we got to the real talk and it was like we shared the same mind. I knew what we had, and you did too. Guess you thought you had control though." Will narrows his gaze, "What are friends for..." He pulls the blade from Chase's mouth with force, causing it to slice down Chase's tongue and bottom lip. His face is a glistening sheet of red, a pretty picture for the two involved. "...except to know how to best hurt someone."

Chase is busily coughing up blood, freaking out at the sight of these new wounds, when Will starts to feel it, the beginnings of the bite.

Onset symptoms are basic, dizzy, sweaty, a feeling of incoming fever. Will notices immediately and casts a full tooth grin, "No way."

Zaff shares the enthusiasm, "I told you I'd show you."

A brand new world begins to unfold, and Will is at the helm of its current point in history. He takes Olivia's idea, "This time I get to choose." Pants pulled to Chase's ankles, he notes the underwear, "Briefs man I see," and proceeds to lower them too.

"He shaves," Zaff says.

"Shaves clean," Will adds.

"Seems…" Zaff tilts his head to one side.

"Yeah, it seems off," Will says. "Like it needs something. Some personality."

Will uses the switchblade on the shaft, cutting deep, from base to the head of the organ. Chase is screaming to the point of going hoarse the entire time. Zaff shakes his head, "Heinous, absolutely heinous."

"Do you regret what you did now?"

Chase can't speak, the pain all encompassing. His penis cut in half, dangling between his legs, looking like a wilted banana peel.

"Hmm?" To Zaff, Will is the alpha, "Do it. Get him to speak."

Zaff raises his arms in defeat, "You got this all under control. You got the power. It's all you." Zaff taps the side of his face, "Get creative. It's going to come back twofold."

A twisted rendition of karma, Will uses this as an opportunity to do a little satisfying torture. How much can a person bleed before the well runs dry? Back to the mouth, he pries some teeth. After the teeth, he cuts along veins, leaves the jugular intact as a failsafe. At some point, Chase will pass out. Will uses the blade in his eye to rouse up to a new height of pain, subsequent lows as he forces him into a doggie style position. Trusty switchblade needing a sheath, he slides it into Chase's asshole while he lets a notable wave of nausea consume him.

"Oh yeah, it's really happening now!" Zaff enjoys the entire moment. "Revenge."

What he doesn't say, and keeps quiet on purpose, is that revenge is never one-sided. It is a reaction to a previous loss, and yet in exerting revenge, it perpetuates a cycle, one where the same hurt and hindrance will come after Will at a later date. It's a curse, and certainly that's precisely what acts as a foundation of this world: a string of curses across time. Zaff has history, so many curses that they've become a living, breathing cancer.

Will is on his way to having that too. The nausea is a viral hello. There's so much it wants to do to you. It hasn't even given him a name. Not yet. Not until the world takes on a new shape, when he starts seeing colors, an entirely new spectrum of energies that make it so that people are revealed for what they are: animals dressed up to be deadly.

With the eye removed, and then a few fingers, there's still more blood to be drawn. Chase is surprisingly still alive as Will finally goes for the jugular. Chase remains alive, feeling everything, by sheer will, cast into reality by none other than the full capability of Will's veracity. Zaff offers a round of applause. Will doesn't hear him and doesn't notice Olivia rejoining them, hoping to have a look. Will takes Chase's life to the brink, to an impossible height of absolute menace, and then he holds on, making every minute feel like a lifetime.

And yet, this all happens in less than 20 minutes.

A glorious moment witnessed by an intimate few. In a blink, Chase remembers everything but is left fully intact, as if he had the most lucid torturous nightmare of his life. Wife walks in and sees him laying on the hardwood floor, completely confused and shouting at the top of his lungs. "Honey, what the hell are you doing?" It isn't a question of concern. Rather, his wife looks at his actions as lesser, inferior, and downright disgusting, "Pull yourself together, come on. We have dinner plans."

The feeling remains constant, Chase in pain with no way of silencing the menace. A curse inflicted upon another, it is Will's way of saying, "may you die a slow and horrible death."

Perhaps in knowing Chase will endure such lows, Will may believe he can move on. He can think so, perhaps even believe it as a real possibility, when really the totality of the situation can be seen at face value. A curse was inflicted, the cycle engaged to repeat ad infinitum.

CHAPTER

XI

Back to the car, back to a less violent world. Give it a minute, and he'll vomit all over the backseat. Zaff sees it coming, much like anyone watching from nearby, any distance safe enough to avoid splatter. Olivia is completely oblivious, and maybe it has more to do with the fact that she knows it's going to be her turn next. The past becomes a wicked present, a dead sprint to a familiar house, and a familiar hate, all because for it to work, for Olivia to join in on the crash, she needs to make peace with the miseries of the past. In its place, only then will she be able to inflict that and so much more, to her heart's (and hate's) content.

Will throws up mostly bile, but there are remnants of his last meal.

"You know you could have, *right?*" Zaff says, watching Will dry heave, the vomit all over his lap and the backseat. He turns to Olivia, "Get any on you?"

She shakes her head slowly.

"You do realize what you did…" Zaff pauses. "Right?"

Will can't quite control his breath. He gags, "I don't want to kill him."

Zaff switches lanes, "Glad you see it. Why blow your load when you can let the pain linger for years."

The car takes on a palpable odor, the distasteful stench of drying stomach fluids, yet they continue driving in silence. The lone spectacle being Will's entry level symptoms. He's enjoying his first foray, introductory steps towards a future crash.

Stopped at a red light, it comes up. Her turn.

"It's your turn," Zaff says, fingers tapping anxiously against the steering wheel.

"I don't know if I can," says Olivia, watching a man at a street corner stumble around, under the influence of an unknown drug.

"Look at him." All attention on Will, clenching his chest. The onset of nausea and fever and it's well on its way to tapping him out for a good 12-hour spell of slumber. "Don't you want to join too?" Will gags, but nothing comes out. His lips have become dried out, chapped from so much stomach acid dehydrating his flesh. A few more upchucks and the area around his mouth will turn pink, borderline red.

Olivia is really missing out.

"Yeah…"

"Well, you got to become friends with your demons, how else will you be able to see what I see?"

There he goes, the vomit more odorous and pronounced. If you were to look closely at what just traveled up Will's throat, they'd see some dotting, proof that the inner lining of his stomach and/or throat could be hemorrhaging. Will falls back against the window, his right hand smearing the window like some future warning.

She looks at the scabbed-over bite, "Is it because…"

"All I can do is show you. You need to see it for yourself."

Olivia runs her finger over the scab, picking at it. The light turns green, Zaff pressing down sharp on the gas, wheels screeching as he cuts a vehicle off, squeezing back into the right lane. She looks back at Will, jealousy rising at the mere sight of him. He's always ahead of her, crashing before she can even show symptoms. How unfair. It dredges up a negative thought spiral, the full extent of it already on the tip of Zaff's tongue.

"So douchebag ex or horrible parents…" Zaff clicks his tongue. "What'll it be?"

Olivia struggles to choose but eventually it loosens itself from some dark corner of her mind, the idea of seeing B again, if only to peel back his skin and see if he really is the monster all these years have made him out to be. Bernard. He doesn't live very far away.

"You're the ghost of trauma's past," Zaff jokes, pointing the sedan towards the suburbs, back to her previous life, away from the various concealable folds of the city, where people pile up and become a crowd to hide in. "Wonder what he'll say first, seeing what's become of you."

This is a turning point of sorts, not just for Olivia but also for Zaff. He's been holding on for a long time. Hold off a little while longer. The attacks worsen, and because he waits until the last possible second, eventually one attack will take too much from him. He'll wallow in the ethers of his subconscious, comatose during the height of what should be the latest spell, another curse upon those that would do nothing but take.

Will is on his way, fading into a deep sleep. He'll stay there in the backseat, enjoying the lethargy.

The drive is somber, Zaff giving way to the sound of the road, engine puttering along the interstate, the signs and the sights becoming increasingly familiar to Olivia, who struggles with memory, all the terrors that history has held onto, still surprisingly fresh, enough that she loses herself to the negative loop.

Zaff eyes her, knowing well that she has gone under, the thoughts swarming and attacking, and he'll do nothing to bring her back to the moment. It's part of what she might need to do, face all that she's held at bay. Meanwhile, Zaff's mentor role continues to rupture along with the incoming failure of his organs, his entire body.

He introduced himself as being terminal.

Soon, sooner than expected, he will introduce the final chapter, the decimating end, which will be the glorious fruit of both Will and Olivia's biggest crash.

The thing about all this is, if you are Will, or you are Olivia, you don't know this until it's spiking your body temperature to 105F. You don't recognize the full picture until you're losing your senses. By then, it's too late. The crash is final, and there's already an entire process that comes along with death. There's always going to be someone enjoying it, every step of the way.

Zaff too. He doesn't see the full picture. He sees more of it, and this "brand new world", it's every bit a power move, a temporary high to the never-ending lows. Zaff enjoys the moment because that's all he really has.

It's her turn.

The ghost of trauma's past sits facing the same single story home, red brick and landscaped lawn, a seldom used basketball hoop in the driveway; it brings up that one time Olivia wanted to go out. With friends! B had called her out, accusing her of having no friends. Then who would she be going out with? It's a similar argument, one that erupts from a lopsided power dynamic. B so possessive of her, even though he had long since lost interest, turning to other women, still desired the need to "own" her. Throughout the argument, B's intention is made increasingly obvious. She cannot entertain the possibility of being interested in someone else, especially a man, one that might become a point of comparison with B. In the mind of B, he worries that he will lose his footing; he will be viewed as less adequate, less of a man. Meanwhile, he produces enough evidence to prove to Olivia that he is far less, each physical strike, cut and bruise added as evidence to further the case of his inadequacy. He doesn't stop there, this lack of confidence extends the altercation to the front lawn, Olivia making it out the front door, only to have B grab her by the ankle. Walking at a brisk pace, only to have a leg caught, it results in a painful fall, her face hitting the sidewalk. The impact is like a cheese grater, her left cheek filed down. B forces her back up, calling her a liar, and that the wound on her face might deter her from fucking some other guy. The final blow, he drags her onto the lawn, tells her she's a slut, and walks back inside, locking and deadbolting the front door.

Olivia relives every painful strike, every demoralizing word.

"This time you'll show me," Zaff says, pulling her away from the memory.

"Yeah," she says.

Zaff removes his belt, offering it as a possible tool, a weapon.

"Thanks," she says.

"Don't thank me. Just get what you need. Better yet, get what you want." He won't be able to hold on for much longer. Underneath the stoic façade, those first tremors have begun to lay claim to his nerves. "Go, before he leaves for work."

She wraps the leather belt around her left fist, "Here goes nothing."

Instead of the front door, she goes around back. From experience, she knows that B leaves the back door unlocked. Zaff gives into the wave, letting the attack hit him full force, and it really does, fully encompassing and frankly destroying his ability to fight back. The worst one yet, his eyes bloodshot, veins bulging in both his neck and forehead, the anguish pops a blood vessel, causing his teeth to tear into his gums, the full extent of the wave resulting in major stress. For a few minutes, Zaff's manufactured persona wilts, and if Will were awake, or if Olivia were to turn around and head back to the sedan, they would see who he really is, a sickly chaser nearing the end of his sprint. If he hadn't inflicted so much hate and destruction throughout his journey, perhaps there could be some compassion. Instead, he is dealt the worst yet, and he rides it out, enduring it all so that he can enjoy the look on her ex's face during his last gasps.

The sliding glass door unlocked; Olivia treats her entry into the home like she had been out running errands. In the kitchen, she helps herself to a glass of water, the belt wound around her left hand, readied for B's entrance.

Gulp, she's so thirsty. Her nerves are flared, the same rush of confidence Will enjoyed during his own vengeance, the same leads Olivia's charge. When B enters the scene, she drops the glass. It shatters, rousing B's attention. She acts it all out, "Oh! You scared me!"

B is dressed in a suit, clearly things have been going well. The business, his machinations, they are all typical. If Olivia cared, she would discover that he had changed career paths, working for a friend's law firm. No need for a degree, or any formal training, not when you're someone like B, networking at a high level, blinding everyone with his candor and charisma. He doesn't speak. Frankly, he doesn't recognize her.

A strange woman, disheveled, matted hair. The stench coming from her, she's a vagrant, homeless. Sickly pale skin, the product of so many names known and conquered, it has made her undesirable to the majority. He keeps his distance as she approaches.

"I went out for a bit," she grins. "Looks like you're off to something big. Where's my big man going?"

Nothing. A blank expression painted across his face, B has both arms behind his back, his back arched and tense. What comes next is altogether natural. She goes in for a hug, and then a kiss, physical affection that causes him to gag, and her to giggle.

"Don't play around like that," she says, unwrapping the belt.

Mid gag, the belt goes around his neck. Before he can undo the hold, the leather strap is fixed in and hooked. She has him on a tight leash where each pull takes more from B, each step digging deeper into the tender flesh of his neck.

Soon he's really struggling, nails digging into the leather belt, B using every bit of strength to get free. Too bad. Olivia went for the stranglehold to sap him of the one thing he always used to dominate and maintain power over her: his physical strength.

"You remember," she whispers, face right up against his. It would be intimate, a romantic notion, if it were in a different context. "You remember how you hurt me."

There's a loud hissing coming from B's mouth. Air escaping from his lungs, he struggles for another breath; all the while, she has her lips on his, taking his breath away. It's a consolation prize, not enough to make up for all that he took, but it's a start.

"I remember," she says. "You liked seeing me writhe. You liked the way it made you feel so damn strong." She giggles, truly high on a surge of confidence, "Big man."

Another pull. B's face is turning purple.

His legs start to go limp.

"I'm just dropping by," she says, watching his face change color. "Wanted to give you a little bit in return for all that you did for me."

It goes on like this for a long while. She doesn't tire of the hold, and she refuses to give him even a moment to come back. By now the belt has broken the skin.

"I'll tell you, in case you forget," she says.

There's so much to talk about, and it takes a long time until the body gives out, giving into strangulation. He falls to the floor, and she drags him into her embrace. Sitting upright with her back against the kitchen cabinets, she reminisces, but instead of letting these traumatic memories claim her, she instead lets them be free to do as they fancy. Next B's arms no longer move, no more scratching or flailing. He's being lulled into confession, not that Olivia desires his confession. What she wants is for him to feel even a little bit of what it felt like to live with him, to be under his control. It was its own curse, a menace she now ensures returns to him in full. While talking about the one time he coerced her for sex while blackout drunk, B's mouth starts to make a strange sound. And then she feels it, the warm liquid. He pisses himself, body releasing the contents of its bladder.

"You remember everything," she says. "To think I trusted you…"

Letting go, there's only a body, left to sit in all its shit and piss. Olivia takes off her soiled clothes, wanting not even an iota of his disgust on her body. She ventures around the house, ducking into the bathroom to take a shower. Afterwards, she discovers a drawer full of women's clothes. Her size. The garments are unrecognizable. Might they be hers?

Zaff is standing near the body when she reemerges from the bathroom.

"It's done," she says, before he can even ask. "Let's go."

End scene.

What a rush, why not visit the family? "It's been years," she says, a lie. It hasn't been nearly as long. Time is what you make of it, and it isn't like Zaff cares about duration. He only cares about how she's taking it right back to the source. The symptoms tick closer like a time bomb ready to waste away all that hurt. Zaff speeds through the suburban streets, both he and Olivia wired and ecstatic, brimming with uncontrollable energy. The world reveals itself, every free lane and every human act, revealed for its want, the take more so than the give, the pain and hurt of millions show themselves at the height of terminal ecstasy like a schematic, an outline that Olivia glimpses for the first (and certainly not the last) time.

It clicks. In the backseat, Will moans, calling attention, to which she says aloud, "Did he see it too?"

"I showed him the world," he nods.

Olivia bounces in her seat, coming apart because there's so much desire and want surging through her entire body. That would be a byproduct of Zaff's latest kick, the attack so ferocious that its aftermath, like any immunity or set of antibodies, gives way to lucidity and euphoria. Olivia doesn't notice the light-headedness, too focused on the house up ahead.

Home bittersweet home.

"I have what I need," she says, preempting Zaff's offering. Olivia gets out of the car while it's still in motion, stomping up the front lawn, using the hide-a-key to gain access. Zaff parks the sedan on the street, cuts the engine, checks on Will, and slips out of the driver's seat.

Zaff approaches the house, gives it a contemplative look, and proceeds down the street, around the corner, up the next avenue, his path diverging once again. As evident and seamless as he had entered Will and Olivia's lives, he exits just as swiftly. The misery that remains, it's what they said they wanted. Now it's a matter of acknowledgment, those first symptoms acting as the first chapter of termination, the biggest power move of all.

It's between family. Olivia finds her father in his office, in the middle of a conference call. She finds her mother upstairs reading a romance novel. Olivia asks if they've been well. In the office, she interjects herself in the video conference call, waving to all of his colleagues, letting slip how he used to hit her until she bled. Mother and daughter pick up where they left off, the fight orbiting details involving where she's been, what she's done, and why Olivia looks so sickly. Olivia has an answer, all rolled into one. After biting her mom on the forearm, much like Will had done to her, she returns to her father, checking in on the unraveling of his career. How about some insurance? She pulls down her jeans, and reveals a long scar on her left cheek. She explains how this is from the time he bent her over and slapped her until she could no longer feel anything. Worth mentioning to the room of strangers that it was done out of disappointment. She wasn't what they wanted her to be, and they wouldn't dare have a child that didn't meet their expectations. Their child. Not a living person, with needs and wants.

"It's okay, though," she grins. "Dad always wanted a daughter to beat."

Such hurtful and horrendous statements, when compared to

what they had told her growing up, pale in comparison to the person they raised. Look at what she has become. This is the product of your parenting. Olivia makes it clear that she has become the full extent of their principles. Father doesn't deserve a bite. Mother tends to the wound, yet without any guidance, she'll succumb to the symptoms without the understanding that she's going to die. She's going to die soon. Her father will want to die, career and marriage set to end horribly.

Olivia stops by her own bedroom, expecting to bring along a bag full of stuff that makes her nostalgic of simpler times. Surprisingly, there isn't anything in her bedroom that she wants. If anything, the sight of the bed, and the oppressive feeling in the bedroom reminds her of all that she left behind. Olivia leaves home one last time. Leaving it all behind, she returns to the sedan, gets into the driver's seat, intent on putting some asphalt between her and the life that is no longer hers.

CHAPTER
XII

The sedan is in motion. Their entire bodies are in motion, a buzzing that introduces the host to its new parasitic strain. There's never a moment when Olivia or Will notice Zaff missing from the picture. Tunnel vision, Olivia driving, speeding down the interstate headed nowhere. Will in the backseat coming to, inspecting the disrepair, the crusted vomit on both seat and lap. There's really nothing to say. He has endured the first symptoms; Olivia is coming down from the incredible high of having done that to her parents and ex. There's so much to enjoy, because this is what she wanted. The feeling of being immune, not to any viral strain, but rather to others. People. The very thing that has commodified both her and Will's lives. The concept of an identity, it has been co-opted by the thought that they are less.

But they are so much more.

They simply have no idea yet to what extent their own journeys will drift and intersect.

Olivia drives without purpose, drifting into lanes, the dizziness beginning to mount. Nausea yet? It'll be there within the next mile or so. Will is weak, perhaps too weak, to do anything but sit there, watching the road.

He drifts along with the sharp right, body thudding against the passenger door. Olivia speeds up, a relic of Zaff's influence, which is much larger than either will ever notice. Zaff walked into their lives only to walk out of it. This was not by chance.

Olivia slams on the brakes, Will's body flying forward, head smashing against the center console. No apologies, she's still way too wired. There's still that nausea about to say hello.

Will doesn't make a sound, the cut on his forehead bleeds, runs down his face. He falls back in his seat, eyes drowsy, he's not seeing the full picture. He is not taking part in the same murderous tunnel vision Olivia has fallen into. No one can be part of her own onset, her personal and private hello. Finally, there it is. Now if only she had a name for it…

Dry heaving quickly devolves into the same clear vomit teased by Will's own kick. Olivia throws up a second time, cloudier, laced with some sort of greenish mucus that makes it difficult to see, the vomit splattering all across the windshield.

After a hello, there is then a need to get to know each other.

What do you do? What are you worth? How may I best use you? They are questions no virus asks, only the living, breathing, mindful opportunist that might decide to take part in what happens next. The car ahead swerves out of the way, seeing two moves ahead. The car behind them, it follows and matches Olivia's increasingly erratic turns of the steering wheel, the stop and go gas and brake resulting from Olivia losing control of her own body.

The driver and passengers of this vehicle, they find in Olivia and Will, that sedan right there about to cause a multiple car pileup, an opportunity. And isn't that how anyone decides to enter anyone's life? They answer those questions even if they don't ever ask. They see in others something they can take.

Her stomach can no longer hold any contents, yet another upchuck reveals a mashing of her last meal, leaving behind severe stomach pains and the introductory lethargy of dehydration. Olivia slams on the gas, sedan speeding up while the vehicle giving chase not only matches the speed but also sidles up to the sedan.

After a moment's look at the severity of Olivia's condition, the driver and passengers see the opportunity, using the vehicle's superior horsepower to overtake and clip Olivia before she can hit the brakes. The sedan's front wheels shift to one side, the bulk of the chassis barreling in the direction of the concrete median. Collision occurs seconds later. The other vehicle continues down the interstate, lowering its speed, merging back into the flow of traffic.

The sedan becomes a dented husk of a vehicle, the latest insurance report complete with bureaucracy hoops that inevitably leads to a hefty bill and payday for somebody. Olivia passed out, cranium pressed against the steering column. Will is somewhere in the backseat, his body crumpled across the vomit crusted pleather.

The scene of the accident holds on like this for longer than any rubbernecker might expect. If an accident isn't called in, or if the others involved stay silent, the wreckage might sit for over a half hour. Think about that, a half hour of people slowing down to rubberneck, get their shock and awe, only to drive onward towards their destination. Think about whom among those rubberneckers might have already cast judgment. Now think of who finally arrives, and what they do with the two human beings hurt, perhaps dying, in the vehicle.

If you think everyone deserves to live, then perhaps one among those hundreds of rubberneckers might have pulled over and done something about it.

Instead, Will and Olivia remain unconscious incubators of their precious newfound symptoms, unable to enjoy the crash because they… crashed. An accident in the truest sense of the term, they are strapped to stretchers, thankfully uncovered, no blanket in sight, and administered to a nearby hospital.

For chasers like Will and Olivia, a hospital is tantamount to a coffin, not a place of recovery.

Immediately diagnosed as terminal, both Will and Olivia are patients in their own curtained little rooms, unconscious and sedated in the emergency room, the beeping of a heart monitor and taped forearms, the IV drip keeping them from greeting death.

What neither will get to experience:

The fact that while they were being driven to the hospital, Will reached the next symptom, the lethargy and dehydration, it evolved into a deadly temperature. That's right, 105F, the same Zaff had discussed perhaps not too long ago.

The EMTs did their best to lower the temperature, the sheer impossibility of his body climbing from a low 100F to 105F before their very eyes, and the fact that it bucked the limits of that temperature, Will's entire body going deathly pale, it's an EMT's worst nightmare.

The fact that his body could be cool to the touch and almost scalding; it all depends on who decides to touch his skin. That anomaly alone would be just cause for delicate moves and a lot of long-term devotion to the study of Will's affliction.

Yet there was more. So much more.

The fact that Olivia's body wouldn't stop vacating its fluids. When the vomiting stopped, it shifted to oozing from her pores, from her nose, from her eyes, a constant tearing that would never be confused for crying. The EMTs were more so distracted by Will's fever, yet the expunging of fluids from Olivia's body was akin to an exodus. Baffled, one EMT could do nothing but watch, going so far as attaching another IV. Fluids in, fluids out.

The fact that in a mere 12-minute drive to the hospital, Olivia's condition caught up to Will's, the onset of fever showing so swiftly, the EMTs had to dig into the reserves, immediately supplying painkillers and higher dosage alternatives in attempt to slow and quash the fever.

However, it doesn't and she's nearing 103.2F when they are finally rolled into the emergency room. EMTs make a huge show of the urgency and severity of this accident.

For perhaps the only time in their lives, Will and Olivia are treated like gold standards, highest priority, if only because they dared to be chasers, and in chasing they caught something new, something right out of a "brand new world."

Silent patients aren't necessarily patients on the mend. The doctors in the ER are clearly baffled by the circumstances: a) it was a car accident and yet neither body exhibits any damage, be it bruises or whiplash and b) the uncharacteristic symptoms that clash and go against each other.

"Where'd he go?"

"He's on another ride."

"Well get him back here."

"But…"

"We need more context!"

A doctor assigned to an impossible file fixates on finding more information. The EMTs finish responding to another call, a stabbing, and a nurse flags one EMT over.

He already knows. "The median crash?"

"Yeah."

"They started showing on the ride here," he shrugs.

"But how?"

"I don't know," the EMT says. "But you better believe we both masked the fuck up."

The nurse frowns, realizing they are navigating the situation blind.

What else is new?

The evening shift consists of a flurry of nurses dropping by to check their temperature, administer different doses, "examine" their progress, or lack thereof. This is clearly a situation where the entire staff can barely contain their bafflement. By morning, they are still unconscious and there is a temporary lull in concern.

A calm before the upcoming storm, a direct result to the high dose pumped through both Will and Olivia's bodies to help allay fever.

A doctor is checking Will's chart, shaking his head, jotting down the current status, temps et al. There's an urgency in his reproach, hinting at a rumor that has begun to spread throughout the department. It has to be something, a new strain? But then what strain? This doctor, like all the other doctors, haven't been able to diagnose their condition. It keeps changing. The worst news yet arrives during this doctor's latest analysis. Right there, between the webbing of Will's fingers, it starts out as irritated looking skin, but in a few blinks of an eye, it's red, puffy.

A rash.

The doctor puts on a pair of gloves, masks up, and gets closer. He lifts and inspects Will's docile, lifeless hand. Between his pointer and middle finger, he discovers what might initially be diagnosed as dermatitis. The dotted rash seems obvious enough.

The doctor proceeds to record the finding, only to see, plain as day, the rash advance, spreading from the sensitive area to the rest of Will's hand. The reddish hue deepens in strength, and it's how it only advances its spread to within a mere inch of the doctor's own grip, seemingly, like the categorization of different buoyancies, avoiding his own fingertips. A mortifying sight, the doctor recoils, dropping Will's hand. The rash continues its spread, the very same area that had donned the imprint of the doctor's fingers is infected, the red, turning almost purple, rash advances up Will's arm.

The doctor calls the name of a nurse, "Quick!"

"Oh my god," the nurse says, stopping dead in her tracks.

The progression of the rash is unlike anything they've witnessed. It reaches Will's neck, and then face, in minutes. His entire body is draped.

The entire staff is frightened.

Perhaps they are unprepared for a glimpse into a world that was always there, they just never had the opportunity to see past the veneer of modern medical science.

"Quickly," the doctor says.

The order is given. Will and the rash temporarily ignored. They flee the room.

Will's body begins to bloat, the skin bubbling in spots, a yellow pus oozing in spots where the top layers of skin are stretched brittle; Olivia's body isn't far off, the beginnings of the same rash form on her earlobes, quickly moving throughout the canal, spreading across her face. For her, it's a spacious dotting of dark red blots, causing it to look like a severe case of chickenpox. Will's body is malformed and disfigured. The rash causes distention. It almost assuredly is violently painful. Too bad the chasers are unable to enjoy it. They are dosed to the point of unnaturally remaining unconscious. This is what they might fear most, to be subjects, test subjects, instead of patients.

Watched from behind a closed door, the hospital staff makes the call.

One of the nurses suggests that "they could be possessed." In the break room, many staffers stick around, too obsessed about this discovery to go home and go about their day. An ongoing open forum of suggestion takes center stage in the room. Between sips of coffee and the occasional bite from a microwaved pastry, they add their comments, circling the same mystery, one that will not be theirs to solve.

"They aren't possessed."

"It does look a lot like demonic possession."

"I don't believe in demons."

"Are you an atheist?"

"I don't believe in anything."

"What about science?"

The room goes silent. A doctor fresh from venturing into the room joins them. Everyone seems to expect an update. The best he can give is, "The guy… it's like smallpox but…"

"How is any of this possible?"

Big question.

Someone has a big answer, "That's what viruses and diseases always show us: We think we know what's possible and then something like a pandemic happens."

The doctor pours himself a cup of coffee, walks over to a nearby wall where he sits down on the floor with a groan.

"18 hours. You should go home."

"No."

"Yeah, neither am I."

"This is ground zero."

"Definitely."

"Does that mean we're all infected?"

Silence.

"Maybe," says the doctor, before sipping the coffee.

"Fuck…"

"Maybe that's how it's spread."

"Through fucking."

"One can hope."

"That's some cruel shit to say!"

"If it's sexually transmitted, it's easier to control than if it's spread through droplets."

There's some consideration among the open forum, eventually leading everyone back to the basic truth. They don't have any clue. It's a mystery. The world remains concealed because they lack the abilities to see any of it, much less an outline.

Someone backs out, "I'm going home."

"I'd wait actually."

"Huh?"

"She should be here soon. She'll tell us if we should all stay put. You know. In case…"

Infection.

For so many the thought of infection accentuates their greatest fears. Yet for a few, the word opens doors. They stay put, the door closed; the worry consumes them, preventing them from seeing the truth to Will and Olivia's crash.

Say it's for the advancement of medical science. Say it's for the betterment of society. Say it's for the containment of a possible deadly virus. Say whatever you want. It all sounds the same. The sound of opportunity is in the air. The CDC sends an epidemiologist; Will and Olivia are prospective patient zeroes relocated and quarantined in their own room.

No one enters without a full body suit.

No one enters, too fearful of what this might be.

The epidemiologist examines their bodies individually with a confidence that is misaligned, yet who would hold it against her? No amount of description would be enough to reveal the terrifying symptoms of this unknown affliction. She grips Will's left arm while she examines his pupils. There, she sees it, just barely. The rash moving, a skittering actually, revealing pale skin where his arm is being held. Slow to react, she spots the odd activity and takes a step back. Olivia is lifeless on her own bed, the rash motionless yet something only the epidemiologist would notice catches her eye. She walks over, noticing how the rash forms and heals in seconds. Once, twice, a third time, she spots multiple dotted lesions on the dermis, forming and fading before her very eyes.

It's all she needs to see. This is going to be huge. For the CDC, for the hospital, for everyone involved. Not that anyone will broadcast the urgency and sensitivity of this discovery, not yet. There's still an opportunity for a few to gain the upper hand. No one wants to share in the benefit if they can have it all for themselves.

Everyone is different and the same should go with their

interactions with a virus. Disfigurement is a symptom, yet Olivia's disfigurement is mild compared to Will's, who continues to suffer from boils and cysts, skin irritation, and a migrating rash that seems to be sensitive to the touch. Medical staff do a few tests, touch and response, and it tracks. Olivia's rash almost immediately dries out, beginning to scab over like a cut. After her skin seems to heal, that's when the seizures and body spasms kick in. The medication being pumped through her body keeps it silent, repressed, and what a shame because they really should have seen it. The painful bursts and radiating waves of pain going up and down arms and legs, just as often originating from the pit of one's stomach before cascading throughout the rest of the body, it's a thing of beauty.

Such an all-encompassing affliction, it's a miracle of a peculiar type.

Her tremors worsen enough that her legs begin to twitch, heart rate increasing dramatically. The medical staff rush between beds, attempting to capture and record every action. Will lets out a moan, audible enough to cause one nurse to scream.

An impossibility of one reality is a constant in another, you just have to understand that reality is checks and balances, concepts accepted and made factual. Here, try this on for size: Will's body improves, the bloating and inflammation deflating. All across his arms and legs, the boils and various protrusions burst, letting out a yellowish-green pus. His body kicks the rash, and though it leaves behind pockmarks and a myriad of blemishes, his body loses the disfiguring expanse. The medical staff is busy inspecting the various blemishes when Olivia, so suddenly, sits up. Full lucidity, she yawns, looks around the room, and then to one of the nurses, "What are you wearing?"

"You're awake," says a doctor.

"My dad probably lost his job," she says.

The nurses whisper, "Look at her vitals."

"I know, I know…"

"B was the worst thing that happened to me."

"Check her dosage."

"I got to say though, I really thought mom would put up a fight. She didn't even try."

Will sits up, a mirrored flash of lucidity.

"I should have extorted 3x as much," he says. Thinks about it and adds, "I should have gone in on it alone."

"I don't know what's happening," says the doctor.

Will and Olivia ignore the medical staff, who react and respond to their remarkable recovery with a sense of unease that borders on unprofessional.

"You really should have," Olivia says. "We could be flying across the country chasing internationally."

"Your dad lost his job," Will says, nodding.

"I know," she grins.

"He sucks, what's-his-name."

"Yeah, whatever," she says.

"And your mom won't make it," Will says.

"She's probably already dead."

CHAPTER
XIII

What are they doing there? Will and Olivia pull the needles from their veins and remove the depressing medical scrubs. Standing before each other, they feel renewed. They just kicked, and the attack is now behind them. Their first attack. It'll be ever present, the crash, ongoing until terminal means death. However, in this moment, both Will and Olivia are feeling euphoric, pristine. Impenetrable. They are invincible. The medical staff, this group of people that try to restrain them, with all their might pinning them back onto their beds, Will has little trouble fending them off with a few elbows and jabs. Olivia matches his motive, kicking and screaming at every attempt they make to pin her naked body to that hospital bed.

It's time to go.

They are really going now. This energy, the veneer of a hospital pulled back, exposing that uncanny world they had glimpsed before, it has never been so obvious. The opportunities are endless, and no human being in this building can make them feel less. Will and Olivia fall into each other, a heartfelt hug, because this is a moment, the moment when it all changes.

They chased and look what they found.

No name for it. Not yet. Not now.

Let them have their light.

The light is so bright, they feel angelic as they turn the aggression back onto the medical staff that had studied them. Somewhere in the mix, the epidemiologist continues to study their condition. This unmistakable affliction, it's going to be her breakthrough. Who cares if the medical staff suffers injuries, perhaps death?

Will takes a needle, the same that had been in his vein, and stabs one of the doctors in the jugular. Swift and straight to the point. He then looks at his arm, noticing the puncture, blood drippage, and with a single swipe of the finger, intent alone closes the gap.

Olivia lands a clumsy knee into the stomach of a nurse trying to strap her to the bed. Turning it on the nurse, Olivia straps her wrists down, leaving her there while she tends to another nurse narrowly close to landing a counterattack.

Both Will and Olivia dance around this most physical scene, but the ending is inevitable. They remain standing, the staff fallen in various states of hurt and harm. The epidemiologist huddles in a far corner, taking notes, hoping she won't be discovered.

"She's probably dead," Olivia says.

"He's ruined."

The lightness, it's all they need. They could have inflicted more across the staff. These are people that sought an understanding for the betterment of their own careers. They racked up a bill that'll never be paid, though the idea was to learn about Will and Olivia's affliction, only to leave them fronting the cost. The CDC would publish a breakthrough study, and the hospital would reap the benefits for being the site of a deadly virus, a Nobel prize winning effort at preventing an incredible evil from cursing the world.

They leave them hanging, unable to do anything close.

There's simply no point. Will and Olivia feel like themselves. They're done with this scene, and they leave the hospital, leaving that epidemiologist to wonder... which just might be the most harmful thing they could have done.

A rare sighting, they walk hands held through the hallways, their bodies pristine, the scarring from the rash no longer present. Outside they choose a vehicle, any will do; how about the SUV over there, second row, third parking spot? It's like this is all premeditated. Olivia drives while Will tends to the radio. They have reason for a soundtrack. It's a celebration.

What does it feel like to be free—from the past, from the hurt, from the ache? This is something to consider as they drive through the town, minding the speed limit, playing into social roles, being "normal" while still carrying the visions of a world pulled apart, bared all, as naked as their own bodies. What does it feel like? They drive into the suburbs, touring the various estates, slowing down to have a look. It's curious at first, nothing more than a glance, until something catches their eye. Maybe they'll try it on for size.

The SUV is parked, and they do all the peeking.

It has nothing to do with the people living in these homes. Will and Olivia tour a home like it's a theme park ride. They open locked doors freely, wandering through rooms, inspecting different pictures and devices. In one home, they lounge on a couch, watching an entire movie. Someone comes home during their viewing, the only reason why Will had to raise a finger. The guy gets pinned to the ground, hog tied with power cords, gagged because he won't shut up.

Curious, they do not desire a curse.

The world naked, seeing all that hurt, Will and Olivia feel… at ease. This might be what it feels like to be a person in a world that makes, in some way, sense. They could get used to this. After the movie, they leave the way they arrived, SUV freely touring the 'burbs.

When they stop to fill the tank up, Olivia goes into the quick mart for some snacks.

It's a scene that would have happened regardless, given the circumstances: a young naked woman. Two men. No watching eye, the employee at the register in the back. They think about it. No doubt about it. Though it seems off, like a trap, they think about it, and because they think about it, Olivia can see how it could unfold. It reminds her of B. It reminds her of those moments when she wanted so much to leave her body, her body often being its own curse. She almost did, once, through a crash that never quite saved her. In this moment, she is saved. She is her own savior.

They try, because of course they try. She leans down, showing. They can't resist.

A few steps and it's like hitting play on a movie you've seen before. The scene goes through its motions, except Olivia isn't part of it. They unknowingly force themselves onto each other. He reaches for the other man's throat at the same time the other man goes for the first guy's groin. Olivia decides on some candy bars and a bag of barbeque chips. For Will. She walks over to the register, waits until the employee returns from the back, and pays.

The employee sees two men individually shopping, one looking for beer, the other skimming the chips section. The scene unfolding for Olivia is purely hers to view, and for both men to feel, the violation incurring is akin to a thought that becomes activated, unable to be erased. It'll preoccupy both men for a long time. Though it doesn't actually happen, the curse is there.

Olivia did it because she could. They wanted to, it was more than a thought. There was evidence of the act, one man moving closer, the other eying her up and down, unable to relent.

They drive through the night, listening to music.

When Olivia gets tired of driving, they pull over, enjoying the remainder of the snacks. They sit and stare at the people coming and going, the rest stop always busy. Every person has somewhere they think they need to be, and yet if they saw the world like they do tonight, people would stop and realize they have all they they'll never need.

"Be safe," he says, watching a young teenager, who just got his driver's license, running back to his hand-me-down Civic. His first road trip.

"Studies show that 87% of new drivers…" Olivia says, as if it's from a song.

They watch and wait for it, and eventually there he is.

"Want to?" Will asks.

The worker he blew, hoping to get an STD. The same sex worker that had been his plan B, a failure, never even once near a crash, he stands near the trucker area, same as always, seeking and hoping to be sought after.

"Let's go," Olivia says.

It's exactly what it looks like. People can't quite believe it. At least one person thinks it's part of a film, maybe there's a camera somewhere and someone's recording. Will and Olivia are lightless, looking the part of being so very perfect and confident. Nobody can touch them, but everyone looks. The guy doesn't recognize Will, even after Will grabs his penis, performing the same act. There's nothing memorable about it. He did it for the money. A transaction. So too will be their interaction. It's a transaction, what happens: Stroke and suck until the point of climax and then stop. Her turn, buildup to near release and then stop. They keep going, and quickly realize this has nothing to do with the worker, who finds the entire prolonged tease excruciating.

They're doing this because they can. They're doing this because it has everything to do with inflicting that curse. When they reach the cusp of the 9th build, the penis beginning to throb, turning blue, the onset of priapism, they stop and identify the meaninglessness of inflicting this curse. Both Will and Olivia stop and look at the organ. They glance at each other.

He nods.

She says, "Let's go."

Back in the SUV, they lose interest in others, instead turning to each other.

"This is what it feels like," she says.

He agrees, "This is what it feels like."

What they don't say: He showed us.

Now they can't unsee what has been fully visualized. Instead, they feel the warmth of the euphoria evolving into its next hour. There's reason to chase it. It becomes selfish, after the traumas and horrors of others carried over time are kicked, washed away, leaving them as two people feeling free, completely unfettered. Their motives become increasingly about him, about her, not even the two of them.

"I could get my job back."

"I'm feeling inspired."

They aren't listening to each other. Beyond their bodies, their minds identify an opportunity. Together, like reciting a poem, they establish what was always true:

"I'll leave when I want," she says.

"We don't owe each other anything," he says.

"I'm using you."

Agreement, an understanding: "I'm using you."

"Give me enough cash and I'll get back on solid footing."

"Give me a chance and I'll show the world."

"Solid footing, I'll spread the curse."

"I'll show them a brand-new world."

Their bond is transitional. Their every pairing, transactional. The rest of the night is a drive back to where they began. The apartment is trashed yet exposed. Back in bed, they hold each other without any physical contact, both bodies under the soiled bedsheets, close, the fabric pressed against skin. They sleep, and it's a dreamless and undisturbed sleep.

The antibody to the first attack, it can last a long time. Each subsequent attack and release, it shortens. If they thought about Zaff, at any point during this entrancing spell, they would see the difficulty with which their paths will criss-cross and eventually collapse.

Yet they are enjoying it.

The light. Through the darkness they spread the curse, yet for a little while, they are immune. They are human immune.

Part Three

HUMAN IMMUNE

CHAPTER
XIV

The thing about the virus is that its purpose is to take. It takes your energy, and then your time, and then finally it takes your life. After Zaff walks away from the sedan, he strolls through the neighborhood, counting the houses, until he reaches the cul-de-sac, the house with the blue door. Turn of the doorknob and he's inside, just in time for another attack. This home belongs to a family, one that might actually know Zaff, though not under that name. There's only one person home right now, and she doesn't seem to notice him watching her as she prepares a meal in the kitchen. A brutal wave of pain sends him upstairs and into a bathroom, where he collapses to the floor as the peak of a wave hits, so painful he goes unconscious.

He stays there, body convulsing, foaming at the mouth, for almost an hour. This isn't going to be the last attack, but it will be the one that begins a strange violent bender of sorts. And it's going to begin with someone he used to know. She might be his sister, or perhaps a close friend from a different era. When Zaff comes to, he is euphoric, wearing the confidence to go back downstairs and greet her hello.

There'll be a moment of surprise, followed by a moment of disbelief. Finally, she will try to stab him with a butcher knife. It leaves a large gash across his face, a perfect visualization, the gash closing on its own before it can let out a droplet of blood.

"Wh-what are you?"

"That's not very nice," he says. "It's me. Can't you see that?"

It's because it's him, not Zaff, but him, the guy that she had loved once, before he broke her heart and changed the way she trusts people for the rest of her life.

"I'm here to apologize," he says.

It could be a lie.

"I don't know how you found me."

How could he not? "I know everything," he grins.

Zaff had to stop by, there's only so much time left, and so he tells her he's dying, and she doesn't seem to care. She doesn't even hear it, instead telling him again, "Get out."

"Not until I've made my point," he says.

What follows is not so much a visage of torture but rather a violent attack using words. Zaff peels back the curtain on the last year of his life, the many names he's used, the virus he is suffering from, the very thing that has made him who he is.

"It's inside me," he says. "At all times. It has shown me a new world."

She shakes her head, not wanting to hear any of it.

"I can show you, you know," he says.

He has to try. They were married once. That was before all the shouting and all the booze. That was when you could say he was normal, job and responsibilities. But where's the fun in that? Zaff wasn't anything but a possible horror story, a glimmer of human cruelty typically saved for fiction. He was just a man, once. Before he spread the curse across the country, he was just a man, spending his days working to pay bills. He hasn't paid a bill in years. Homeless, preying on the misguided kindness of others, and the hurt both inflicted and dealt, Zaff has followed a path of destruction. It's a path that's finally ending.

"It doesn't have to be about goodbyes," he says.

Using the same butcher knife, he chops off three of his fingers, placing them on the counter, so that she can watch them bleed. Wait for it, wait for it… he lets the blood pool and then he takes the fingers, reaffixing them to his hand. He doesn't show any signs of pain. He's felt all there is to pain, the worst of it. He has only a few attacks left to endure. The veneer of confidence will send him to the floor, crawling on his hands and knees, soon enough.

"You're the worst thing that's ever happened to me," she says, a sheet of tears dampens the front of her sweater. "I almost forgot you existed."

"I exist," he nods. "There isn't any doubt that I exist. I'm more unique than you think."

He grabs her, pulls her close. She fights him, landing slaps across the face, a kick to the groin. Takes it all, nothing's going to slow Zaff down.

"You remember when…" he describes their wedding night. "Our vows…" he goes into detail about the custom vows they read aloud during the ceremony. "You promised…" It's something they never got around to doing, and now, with so little time left, he wants it. "If you play it right, you just might get something back."

He gets what he wants. It's not what she thinks. There's little interest in sex; Zaff's thinking about something else. Just a taste. The knife is used to cut her, tapping into a vein, he wraps his lips around the area of the cut, lapping at the warm coppery liquid. Taste it. It's so warm. After a mouthful, he swallows and grins, the cracks between his teeth red from her precious blood. She can't control herself, body beginning to shake. So upset, she says things like "my kids will be home soon" and "I can't believe this is happening."

"It's happening," he says, drinking more of her blood. "We're role playing. I'm a vampire and you're giving me life."

What she doesn't realize is that he's giving her the same affliction. It'll be a little while, eventually she'll have an emotional experience, which will trigger the dormant virus, sending her a caustic list of symptoms, changing her life for what little time she'll have left.

"A gift," he says, when he's finished.

She doesn't understand.

Letting her go, he walks to the front door and stops, "You know, I wasn't the worst thing to happen to you. Remember Christmas 1993?"

Her bottom lip quivers. It looks like she had forgotten, or rather it had become lost to the weight of so many memories. Something like that, it feeds on a person's brain. It will likely be all she thinks about, the topic of next week's therapy session, and the trigger needed to engage with this terminal affliction. Zaff's insurance policy activated, he leaves her life so that this can end the way he always knew it would end.

Zaff drives to the airport and gets on a plane. His destination is another city. It could be that he knows he's being followed, or that he wants to take the curse to a dense crowd of people. Whatever the motivation, he's on a plane, pretending to sleep, when the next attack happens. He rushes into the aisle, nearly falling onto someone, the flight attendant helping him up.

"Sir, are you okay?"

"Well that's..." he mumbles, "a loaded question."

He locks himself in the tiny plane restroom and sits on the seat. Dry heaving, he's a bit shocked at how the attack is different. The waves of pain have been swapped out for nausea. It's like the affliction is regressing. It's more than a little odd. Zaff has gotten used to understanding the routines of the affliction. A person can get used to anything, even a terminal illness that slowly destroys them from the inside out.

An attempt at throwing up yields nothing. He shoves his fingers down his throat. Still nothing. The nausea brings along a decimating amount of paranoia. Could this be it? The final attack. The odds are stacked against him. Unclear how long he is in the restroom but eventually there's a knock. Must have been long enough that the flight attendant checks on him.

"Sir?"

He clenches his stomach. "What the fuck is going on…"

Another knock. "Sir? Hello? We're landing."

When he looks in the mirror, he's in for a nice surprise. Confirmation that things have indeed gotten worse. His skin is ghost white, the color drained; his eyes are bloodshot, and his lips are purple.

"Wow," he says, widening his eyes.

"Sir?"

If this is the attack, there's no telling if or when the full-bodied pain will kick in. The nausea is constant, though. It turns out to be more debilitating than any ache. The paranoia keeps him locked in the restroom. The way he looks prevents him from celebrating. Though it's exciting, this is all so new; he does carry a palpable sense of worry.

Bouts of vertigo, another symptom of the attack. It'll make it difficult for him to walk anywhere. He's drunk, some might say. Others might say, That guy's a wreck. The latter might be true. One thing's clear, he isn't leaving the restroom. More voices join in on the check-in. They grow concerned that he might be hurt. The silence carries along until they give up, the plane deboarded and in the midst of being cleaned.

He'll leave the restroom, coast clear, nobody but the cleaning crew, who take one look at him and back away. Keep your distance, that's right. It's like he has the force to keep people from being a bother. The entire journey through the airport, people move out of his way, parting like a sea. He falls a few times and has the bruises to show for it. Another new occurrence: The wounds remain. No amount of trying will undo any damage dealt to his body.

No use trying to hail a cab, he walks to the parking lot and discovers the occurrence extends to other objects too. The doors won't unlock. He isn't able to gain access to a vehicle. It's as though the affliction is fading. Could it be that he is on the mend?

That's the real fear.

He decides on using a driving app.

The driver that picks him up doesn't want the fare, "No. No. Get out."

"Just... drive to the location," he says, laying down in the backseat, a full and decimating exhaustion kicking in.

"No," the driver shakes his head. "Fuck no. You, get the fuck out!"

It's a stalemate. The driver drops the ride, and when he can't seem to get a response from Zaff, who has fallen asleep in the backseat, the driver forces him out of the vehicle. Zaff wakes up when the driver grabs him by the shoulders, and he manages to land a hefty kick to the driver's left knee. Struggling for some strength, Zaff jumps at the driver, both crashing to the concrete with a loud smack. Zaff crawls on all fours, makes it to the driver's side before the driver can, and with another strike, this time to the face, the driver falls back, letting out a painful groan. Zaff gets behind the wheel and drives off.

He has trouble staying awake. In multiple instances, he nearly causes a pileup. Still, he must persevere! Through the height of city traffic, Zaff keeps driving, a destination forming in his mind. Over the bridge, he makes it into the touristy section of the city. At a stoplight, his tired, bloodshot eyes watch a crowd of people, many of them dressed similarly, cross the street. They are all wearing green and red, festive attire. It must be some kind of holiday. Zaff wouldn't know. The attack devolves to include heart palpitations. The erratic skip and steady tremor of his veins, blood seemingly reaching boiling point, it causes even more confusion. Fever? Now?

Zaff doesn't know where he's headed until he's already there. The large tree decorated and glowing with hundreds of lights, it's impressive, an icon of gratitude and giving. Too bad Zaff enters the picture, stumbling forward and falling to his knees.

"Oh shit, you okay, bud?" A young man comes to his aid, hands grabbing his arms only for him to pull back, "Fuck."

Scalding to the touch, Zaff shows his face and the young man can't run away fast enough. This is how it's going to be. He must realize that if this is the attack, it is almost definitely the one that will never let up. Back on his feet, he takes a few steps, looking up at the large tree, then he takes in the various displays of holiday cheer.

A couple poses for a selfie behind the tree, even though there's no way the phone camera will capture the entire tree.

A family of four, two kids, struggle to get the right stance, a professional photographer taking the shot.

A man gets down on one knee, a marriage proposal. His partner, and likely fiancée, so emotional, it's something that Zaff cannot fully comprehend.

A woman busy texting on her phone is sidelined by another friend. They shout and cheer and hug and it's a reunion. People can care so much about each other.

A man with a camera films a woman dancing in front of the tree.

Always, the tree. It stands for something.

Zaff gazes up at it a second time.

Then it clicks. This is it.

He chokes, coughing up blood.

The blood jets out like vomit, splattering the area at his feet. The crowd reacts with fear, people equally shocked. The disbelief draws a crowd, even after Zaff throws up again, more blood.

Oh my.

He's sick.

Look at all that blood.

Someone should do something.

Words without attribute, the crowd gathers closer, as if attempting to quell the chaos. And yes, someone should do something. Perhaps someone already is. They are merely biding their time. Timing is everything. Zaff seems to gain a second wind, the bloody vomit leaving him feeling better, enough to wave to the crowd, "Bad sushi."

Still has a sense of humor. Good to see.

It won't last. Zaff is slammed with a bad bout of vertigo, causing him to lean forward, almost a fall, only to twist his ankle as he collapses to his side.

"I'm such a mess," he says to himself.

Never, not even once, does he blame the virus. If there's any blame, it's in the fact that he doesn't get any more time. Worse, the curse it seems has only one last victim, himself.

Once it becomes clear how it's going to end, Zaff gets on with last rites. Scanning the area for possibilities, he finds a container of gasoline near one of the nearby generators. A man smoking a cigarette near the curb, Zaff stumbles over, dried blood caked to either side of his mouth, "Got... a light?"

Zaff doesn't wait for the guy to react, invading his personal space to retrieve the lighter from the man's pockets. Back to the tree, he looks up at it, pretends to smile, and then feels a burning hot vile vomit on the rise. It's the worst one yet, the bloody concoction goes airborne, almost reaching the crowd. They've got their phones out. The footage will end up online. It'll land on the news, no doubt about it. He wipes the blood from his mouth on his forearm, looks at the blood, smears it across his face.

So be it.

He gives himself a gasoline bath.

Lighter in hand, the signature snap right before a sudden spark, Zaff's entire body going up in flames. Nobody tries to put out the fire, and Zaff doesn't make a peep. He falls to his knees, looking up at the Christmas tree. The last thing he sees, he is a dying corpse stinking up the area. By the time anyone is there to tend to the mess, Zaff will no longer exist. The man that was Zaff will no longer have a curse to contend with.

This is the part where his story ends, and yet some of the most important details are given during the aftermath.

The EMTs and cops arrive to contend with the media swarming the horrendous sight. The area around the scene is marked off with tape, like it was a homicide. The authorities call in extra help when someone tries to get to the body. It isn't just one person either. There are four of them and they approach the body with purpose. One member causes a distraction, willingly allowing possible arrest, while the other three head for the smoldered mess of Zaff's body. A member doesn't seem to mind the burns, getting a quick in-depth inspection. This is all an interesting development, should the crowd notice. Though a few do, the majority of the attention is cast towards the decoy, who has a number of options. When the trio takes longer than expected with Zaff's body, the decoy pulls out a gun.

"What the fuck is happening?!" Someone shouts, and it accurately describes the events happening that night, at the unlikeliest of crime scenes. The trio seems disappointed, like they were expecting more, and retreat, each leaving the body for a different direction. The decoy drops the gun and leaves. The authorities follow and the decoy starts running.

It's all caught on numerous cameras, not that any of this footage goes anywhere. Perhaps it's snuffed out. The reason remains unclear. However, the facts remain the same: Someone self immolated in front of the city's legendary Christmas tree. Reports from witnesses claim that the man "was unwell" and "looked deeply hurt." One witness testimony claims he "was a broken man and was suffering." The official story, the one that proliferates itself across the news, discusses a Roderick Halverson, age 29, and how he had been a computer programmer before a lengthy divorce resulted in him quitting his job. Everyone that knew him said they lost touch around the same time. Halverson seemingly disappeared the moment he lost it all. Online, some threads exist about Halverson, claiming all kinds of things. People dig up his criminal record but all they can find are a few DUIs. Someone mentions the trio inspecting the body, but it doesn't get a whole lot of attention. It's worth mentioning here though, just like it's worth mentioning elsewhere how neither Will nor Olivia are around to hear of Zaff's demise.

For all they know, he's still out there, occupying a space in a *brand-new world*.

CH~~APTER~~

XV

In the morning, Olivia leaves the apartment. Will doesn't need to say anything. After the euphoria of the latest crash, they both understand, and there's no use trying to put it into words. In fact, she wants to leave. It's what she desires most. The lightness of feeling, she can't stand the newly oppressive atmosphere of the apartment. So she wakes up, puts on some clothes, and is out the door—out of his life—before dawn.

Will pretends to be asleep, watching her leave.

He should feel something about this, forlorn or at least a little sad. Instead, he feels nothing, much like how Olivia doesn't pay any heed to this moment. There's so much to gain, a world of opportunity, when one feels invincible, steeled against anything that can be inflicted upon themselves by others. Sticks and stones but they've got steel.

Thinking about it, perhaps there's something to mark the occasion. He checks and notices that he has a slight erection. Maybe that's the best choice, masturbating to the thought of Olivia off in the world, the brand-new world, inflicting her own curse across all those that would easily do the same, if they had the means. He falls asleep to the idea, body going limp.

It's well into the afternoon when he wakes up.

What day is it? A Tuesday.

Will showers and gets dressed. He finds a blazer, dress shirt, and pants in the closet, surprisingly clean, untouched by their years of filth. Looking the part, he leaves the apartment, preferring to be driven rather than drive. While waiting for the driver, he calls the landlord.

"You got the rent? Back rent too?" he says.

It gives the landlord some pause, "Excuse me?"

"You have. The rent. We're caught up. Good?"

After some hesitation, the landlord clears his throat, "Yeah, yeah we're good."

"Can you get a cleaning service in the apartment, today please? I'll pay. Seems someone tried to trash the place."

"Oh that's no good. I know a good crew. Cool if we let ourselves in?"

Amazing to see how swiftly the treatment and tone shifts, suddenly treated with respect, if only because of the aftereffects. Will carries himself well, confidence and certainty, to any unsuspecting individual he seems like a shining star, when really it has more to do with him having the world in the palm of his hands.

"Good," he says, ending the call.

The car pulls up, the driver offering niceties, Will's not really interested. It's more about getting to the address given. Will has ideas, and they will fully form as he reaches the building, the headquarters for a competing company. If his employer of so many years called him a fraud, he will just have to offer his full range of expertise to their leading competitor.

In the lobby, he flirts with the receptionist. No reason or motive, other than to get what he wants. That's what it's about, isn't it? Getting what you want.

"I have an appointment," he says.

Symptoms of the next attack begin to form out the corner of his eye. It's like electricity, pulling at his vision, elongating it, and making it difficult to concentrate.

"I'm sorry, you're not showing up in the system. Let me see what I can do," she grins, apologizing a second time.

He sits on a nearby couch, working on maintaining his cool. This is new, the attack's symptoms. Like Zaff speaking to him through hurt and ache, he recognizes that all that confidence, the euphoria, the world he sees disappears behind a sheet of doubt and despair. During the worst of the attack, he mustn't let himself get carried away. This means he should probably find somewhere else to be right now.

Falling into place, he rushes, where else, an empty conference room, an elevator all his own, anywhere. The receptionist calls to him, but he isn't paying her any attention. Blood flows from his nose, his head is throbbing…

Here it comes.

The best he can do is an elevator going up, two employees there, frightened to death as he endures the height of the attack. It only lasts a few minutes, but it's enough to scar both bystanders for life. Firstly, the blood from his nose. Secondly, bulging veins, dry heaving, a full-bodied painful attack. Everything is so new, he doesn't have much of a tolerance, which results in copious amount of grunts and screams. Splayed across the floor, he wipes blood from his ears and eyes. They watch, two strangers suddenly huddled in a corner together. Will wipes away all the blood, only for another outpour to trickle from his tear ducts. The pain feels endless, yet the attack only lasts the duration of the elevator passing between floors.

A chime followed by the doors sliding open, Will is already on his feet, reddened yet newly confident. The attack pushes, and Will pushes back. The bystanders rush out of the elevator. He must have chosen to keep the memory alive instead of washing it clean. Though he does wash clean any trace of his body fluids. The blood is gone, and he's back to that same charismatic glow. There's one person looking to board the elevator.

"Going down?" He asks.

He nods, steps into the elevator.

Will presses 1 for the lobby. Back to it.

"Thanks."

"Think nothing of it." Surely, Will won't.

The receptionist remembers him, "I was just about to go find you!"

"Sorry," he winks, a mimicry of Zaff's own mannerisms. "I had to take an important call."

She bats it away, "Think nothing of it. Kelso will see you. 15th floor, just tell them I sent you."

"And your name is?"

She blushes, "It's Amber."

"Well then, Amber..." And it's one of those flirtations, a transactional exchange wherein he gets to feel in control, and Amber gets to feel wanted, desired, and most of all, paid attention to, when most days she's nothing more than a body at a desk, people barely even acknowledging her as a human being. Numbers are exchanged, and in Will's mind there's another idea sprouting. If she's lucky, he thinks, maybe she might crash too. Grab a bite, maybe get a bite...

On the 15th floor, a man in a blue suit meets him in the hallway.

"Will?"

He turns, adapting on the fly, "Yes. You must be Kelso."

"So nice to meet you," Kelso offers his hand.

A nice strong handshake. The sort that adds to a first impression. Not that Will needs any help. He's lighter than when he arrived. The whole interaction plays itself out five steps ahead of actuality. Kelso will walk him to his own private office, all the while chatting Will up for details, not that Will gives any. Not yet. Kelso will let slip that he knows about the fraud, but also finds it compelling, because it proves that Will can reverse engineer anything. Will takes it in stride, again, offering no details. Leave the mystery alive; let it give him control over the entire exchange. When they're finally in Kelso's office, Will seated across from him, they get to talking. "You probably understand why I'm here," Will says.

Kelso, hands folded, leaning back in his chair, playing his part. He's the boss here, examining Will, not the other way around. Yet, already there's a shift happening, in both control and confidence. "I think I have an idea."

Will grins, "I figured." He leans forward, placing both hands palm up. "There's a thing so seldom used. Trust. In this business, in any business. People think about their profit margin and they think about their bottom line, but few ever really think about trust."

"Trust is hard to come by," Kelso says.

"In my past, trust was always the first to go. I placed my trust in the wrong hands. They took," Will clasps his left hand shut. "And they took again," right hand shut. He raises both fists into fighting stance. "They left me with no other choice than to fight."

This seems to entice Kelso, who raises his fists too.

Both in fighting stance, Will asks, "Are you going to fight me?"

The words are placed in Kelso's mouth, "Only if you want a fight."

Will stands up.

Kelso follows his lead.

The desk between them, there's no way to land a hefty blow. Will directs the entire scene, Kelso throwing the first punch. He lets it land on his right cheek. A counter attack, Will lands a body shot, Kelso buckling with a laugh. "Nice."

They trade blows until Will has found his point. Kelso breaks a sweat, a little out of breath. Will sits back down, Kelso matching each move.

"It can be a lot worse," Will says, a warning.

Kelso doesn't understand.

Will spells it out for him: "Here's what you're looking at, and then I'll tell you what you're looking for. You know I've been indicted for fraud. I have a record. I'm unable to work for any company because I've got that black mark on my CV. Still, what I do have are the keys to the proverbial city. I know how every company's pipelines work, and I can navigate any level of encryption. There's going to be a crash. The entire market will suffer. No company will be left unscathed. They are out there, learning everyone's pipelines. It's only a matter of time before they mastermind their attack. You'll be fast asleep one night, thinking everything in the world is right, or at least everything in your world is going well. Then you'll wake up and it'll be a trash fire, everything will be lost, including your job. Your life will take a dark turn. Are you ready for that kind of fight?"

What is there for someone like Kelso to say? Under Will's spell, he hands him everything he asks for. A six-figure starting salary, an office next to Kelso's. An executive position, and enough leverage to "get the job done." Confidence running high, Will engages in a handshake, sparing Kelso from any further spells, and bids him a good day.

"See you tomorrow!" Kelso says, a big smile. "Welcome to the team!"

"Glad to be here," Will says, that same wink.

When he returns to the apartment, it has been fully restored, carpet deep cleaned, the bathtub bleached, even the mattress and bedsheets cleaned. It looks and feels like a brand-new apartment. It's… a brand-new world. Will orders some Thai food and watches TV while waiting for it to arrive. There's a moment where he feels a little off, recollection of a time not too long ago when he and Olivia were on the same couch, chasing and failing to find a lead. Look at how quickly things change. Dinner is okay, who really cares. He eats and tosses most of it away. Not much of an appetite, he's going to endure yet another attack.

This time he can sense it on the horizon.

"God, not again."

Feeling the sudden onset of fever, he removes his clothes and gets into an ice bath, an attempt to parlay the symptoms, perhaps the cold temperature jolting enough of his extremities so that he can curtail the next attack.

"The hell is it…" He wonders what he has. There's no name for it. It gives as much as it takes. The crash is one thing, the euphoria another… but it seems to have a mind of its own. It wants all of him, and Will at his lowest, he begins to question what Zaff had given them. He shivers in the cool water, but his body temperature holds, thawing the ice, in under 20 minutes, leaving the water more lukewarm than cold.

He remains in the water, feeling helpless.

And then the waves of pain, so iconic of the virus, begin their attack on his senses. It's the nerve pain that hurts the most. Some waves are so alarming, he temporarily loses his sight. Everything goes cloudy and dim. He cries out, "Help…!"

No one is going to help you.

He must endure the attack alone. Nerve pain lasts about 10 minutes. He will start to fall asleep, all that pain really sapping his strength, only to get another wave of pain, this time his muscles twitching and spasming, convulsing to the same rhythm as his heartbeat. Holding his breath, he tries to slow his heart, thereby lessening the hurt, but it's no use. This will hurt him and it will leave him feeling completely numb.

Falling asleep in the tub, he pisses himself at some point, the water turning a light yellow. Waking up after a good hour submerged in spoiled water, he shivers and falls out of the tub. His skin is disgustingly pruned. He doesn't have enough energy to make it to bed; he goes for the blanket, pulls it partway, and falls into a deep sleep on the floor.

He wakes up feeling light, impossibly confident.

Shower, shave, a fresh new outfit: Will checks himself out in the mirror.

Today is his first day, a new life. What will he inflict upon others? Shall he dredge up past traumas of his own, handing them off piecemeal to his colleagues?

The morning standup. He counts a half dozen colleagues working in Kelso's department. Cybersecurity is their priority, a key component to the company's standing among the further expansion of cryptocurrencies and investments. It's all jargon for a simple and all-encompassing need: to be protected. Will is introduced by Kelso after his morning ramble. Will is glowing, everyone already looking curiously in his direction before he finally gets his chance to speak up.

"Hello," he waves. "You probably already know me."

They do. Many of them wouldn't dare mention how they came to learn about Will and his illegal activities.

"If you do, great, saves me some explanation… but if you don't, well, then I guess we're going to have to go through it bit by bit, hmm?" He speaks like he should be Kelso's superior, and as he discloses his criminal past, the extortion and everything that should have led to a person's life fully ruined, he changes the narrative, claiming a second chance, a new prowess, and most of all a boastful declaration. "You need me."

First up it's Kelso. "You need me because you're in over your head. How you became head of the department, it probably has to do with sleeping with the CEO. Oh, but nobody knows about that, right? Whoops! Anyway, you landed the job because Harry's infatuated with you."

Next, he turns to a random employee. Instantly he knows everything, demons exposed. "You…" the employee shakes his head. "I said you, you might want to stop digging into those dark web URLs. You're feeding an unnatural interest. Get some help."

Turning to Kelso's assistant, "And you, how much longer will you remain at this shitty position before you finally give up and go chase your dreams? Enough petty stealing. No one has noticed you stealing office supplies, reading their emails, whatever. It's like you want to get caught but because it's so petty, no one even notices."

To another, he grabs the guy by the shoulder, "You really need to kill it with the drinking. It's bad. Real bad. Do you remember what you did last night? Didn't think so. That's the sort of shit that comes back to haunt you. People you hurt, people you fucked. Things you did during black out…"

And then it's a shy guy with glasses, one of the engineers, someone he will be working with often, "I bet we're going to see a lot of each other, so maybe I'll keep this quick. Not too expository, but wow, just wow. How did you get away with it? I guess with enough money from mom and dad, you can get a good lawyer that can make it so that even 'accidental murder' can go away. But I don't know how you can live with yourself…"

In this world, everything is paper thin and obvious. The petty seeking pleasure, the majority addicted to power. Humanity might be the blanket term, but in this reality, every single being is looking out for only themselves.

It's Zaff talking through him, Will falling into place, the provocateur and the one fully in power. Being at the center, it's beyond blissful. You see everything for what it really is, and all you want to do is destroy it. Destroy it all. This was all a mistake, and you want nothing more than to ensure that the curse extends across the entire known world, so that maybe the survivors can start anew. The world can end, and another can begin. Let there be a collapse, so that creation can tell a new story, where those that are birthed do better. They are not there to spin their own selfish narratives. They are there to exist in a capacity greater than any human being.

Or maybe not, so Will lures them into traps, linguistic pitfalls, and watches as the department turns on each other. Verbal fights become vicious attacks. Three employees attack Kelso, pinning him to a nearby desk. One female employee takes a pen and stabs someone in the eye. One must imagine more than impulse led to such an attack. All around Will, the department buckles against a heated wave of chaos. He stands tall at the front of the room, enjoying the sight. The curse upon them, they are his colleagues. When it goes too far, likely when Kelso is being electrocuted, he will take things a step back. Everyone remembers, but there's no evidence of any carnage. They blink and suddenly it's all a bad dream, one that hangs there, making the days and weeks to follow uncomfortable. Notice anything?

They will be kinder to each other, walking on eggshells, embarrassed and ashamed by this nightmare that won't leave. Colleagues act like civil colleagues. Kelso takes everyone out to dinner, a "bonding exercise," on the company's dime. Department morale increases. Everyone enjoys their workdays… for a little while.

Will is too preoccupied to enjoy his work.

There'll be another attack, and though he is unwilling to admit it, he's becoming afraid of the future. Every attack offers something new, yet it requires so much of him. Soon there won't be anything left.

CHAPTER
XVI

When Olivia leaves the apartment, she knows exactly where not to go. "Never again," she whispers. Never again, the house, the home, the concept of friends and family. Never again, they won't ever see her again. Never again, she thinks, picking out her dream car, echoing Zaff's motivations; her willingness enough to claim a convertible as her own. It's all she ever wanted, or at least for as long as the road keeps her entertained. She speeds down the interstate, chasing the feeling of being free, of being herself. The euphoria will last long enough to give her a window into how this will work. The city is calling, and she doesn't need to answer to conquer what remains in her sights.

This is what it feels like, she must think, after she gets used to riding the left lane, the music turned up high. This is what it feels like to be a person that is in control of their thoughts and actions, emotions and memories. There are no hurdles, and no more fears. This is forever, this feeling of being herself. It's the first time she isn't chasing anything. There are no symptoms claiming her consciousness. The only thing to claim is the open road. Trees rolling past blend together with possibilities. Does she take that exit or the one ten mile markers from now?

Possibilities.

Olivia has never had so many possibilities.

"I love this song," she says, turning up the volume. It's a song from her past, though she doesn't recognize the artist, only the rhythm. She hums along to the beat, pushing the convertible to the limit. If she weren't riding the euphoria, she may have crashed into that semitruck. Instead, she switches tracks, something heavier, more decimating to match her mood.

"I could have been a musician. I knew someone that really wanted to start a band. He played guitar. I don't remember if he was any good… but he got a band together quick. His friends. They had an audition. I can't believe I tried out. Bass and then vocals. They liked that I was a girl. I remember him saying that a female fronted band would cut through the noise. They looked at me like I could add to their potential. They didn't really even have me sing. I tried out and was their vocalist. After a few practices, where they basically just talked about being a band instead of playing, they stopped calling. I hit them up via text, but nothing. Turns out they broke up. One of them went on and started another band. I don't remember any of their names. The guy that started another band though, last I heard they were playing shows. Real shows. It's all such a distant memory now. I think back and all I can remember is them looking me up and down and asking if I'd be into 'going haute goth.'"

The half memory hangs there, before slipping away, carried off at 85MPH.

"I could have been a writer. I always kept a journal as a kid. Yeah, I used to write every day. About the day, about my dreams. It wasn't a dream journal because I wrote it out like it was a movie. I have always liked the way movies can feel like suspended time. I wrote about my imaginary friends, back when I had imaginary friends… I wrote about my friends. The people I thought were my friends. I never wrote about my family. Hmm, I guess it's because I didn't want to make my writing seem mean. It was a fun thing, practicing my penmanship while also telling a story, though it was really only a story for myself.

She can see the buildings in the distance. Almost there…

"I could have been a teacher. A professor, it just sounds awesome to be referred to as a professor. Like you have knowledge that becomes your duty to impart onto others. That's what I think I like so much about the idea of being a teacher: You want to… help people. It's not about taking something from someone. It's about giving to others and not worrying if they're taking too much because it's the job. It's part of the job—you know what you're going to give. They get to learn, or they don't. It's always been nice, the idea that someone is valued for their mind.

There's more traffic the closer she gets to the tunnel leading into the city. Forced to slow down, she switches lanes, taking the middle one, desiring no road rage or people giving her a hard time. It's a smooth ride, even in traffic, the angst and stress of drivers on all four sides muted as she continues to reflect, each memory deflected as it makes its last attempt.

She cuts someone off and it's like the vehicle isn't even there. A swift turn of the wheel and she's where she wants to be. That exit, that's where she's going.

The car takes her through the outskirts of the city, each block revealing its outline, the blueprint of social norms and activations, everyone acting according to their needs and desires. Olivia is struck by how people can be so blind, adapting to any conditions. Play it as it lays. There's someone on the street corner, under the influence; he's being spotted by three men sitting on a nearby stoop. They're thinking about it. Olivia can see how it'll unfold, and in a brand new world, it ends with the inebriated man stripped of his wallet and any valuables. In a brand new world, it could be so much worse, the trio with the power has their choices, but who nearby might be there to complicate their options?

Olivia is on another block, seeing behind closed doors countless individuals in varying states of undress. It's night, for many they are looking to retire for the remainder of this day. Let there be another, perhaps, yet for Olivia, this is just the beginning.

"I still can," she says, a smile forming across her face. "What do I want to show them?"

This is the part where she ditches the vehicle, leaves it for someone to find. They're not going to find her. It's the part where she gets a studio apartment, able to sign a lease without any proof of employment. She uses every sheen and shimmer of the tail end of the euphoria to secure a spot in the city, a home to call her own. She lives right across from the park. It's a new day and she hasn't slept a wink but there she is, a studio apartment all her own to fully furnish.

She lies down on the hardwood floor.

It's going to happen. The next attack. It's different for her, a spout of vertigo. When she tries to stand up, she falls back down on the floor.

"Wow," she mumbles. Easy enough to disregard it as exhaustion. She did just drive 14 hours, stayed up all night, and forgot to eat. When it doesn't kick, and she's left on the floor, unable to move without seeing dots, feeling borderline nauseous, she breathes out and begins to understand, quicker than Will was able to navigate, the onset of something new.

Olivia settles into the symptoms, acknowledging what must be endured before she may arrive at her next destination. Motionless, her body begins to surge, waves of heat without the pain. Keeping an eye on her skin, Olivia seems to expect a rash, kind of like before, but there's nothing. After an hour, the heat flashes stop. The vertigo isn't as bad, and she's able to stand up again. After a few stretches, it looks like she's past the worst of it.

Not bad at all, she takes another tour around her apartment. Her apartment.

It still doesn't feel like reality. In her vulnerable state, Olivia is unable to fight back the paranoia dealing with being found out. She's all alone in this city, penniless, no prospects. She looks at the street below, crowds gather while others disperse between destinations; who might have her name? Who might once again prove to her the capability of others to take, and destroy, and worst of all, demean all that she desires to become?

Then it hits her, and she rushes to the bathroom, just barely making it in time. Throwing up a pinkish substance, her stomach tremors with ache, taking her legs, another bout of vertigo causing her to crack her skull against the porcelain.

Gone, but not without the anguish, Olivia wakes up minutes later feeling better. She feels the area where her skull has been split. It feels jagged, like shark teeth; pressing her palm against the warm and sticky wound, she is reminded of how Zaff cut his hand, only to quickly undo it from possibility. Her skull is preserved, along with the feeling of invulnerability.

Ready, she walks out the front door, locking it shut.

Leaving her apartment. Walking down her street. She gets a lay of the land, the street corner bodegas and nearby coffee shops. The atmosphere of a neighborhood that just might be that, neighborly, enough in a city sense of the term. There are no helloes and everyone keeps to themselves. The way she likes it. For the first time ever, she walks a sidewalk without worry of walking too slow, taking up space. She scans the storefronts for things that might call to her.

It could be that it finds her, the modest and clean storefront, lacking any name. She stands before the floral depictions, not quite sure what this store is advertising. Then it hits her, it isn't a store at all. Between portraits, she glimpses the rest of the gallery. The walls are spaciously decorated, each piece given ample space. There's only a lone desk in the back, a man in a fashionable shirt and platinum colored hair sitting at it with his feet up, phone in hand.

Interestingly, Olivia pursues this endeavor. Art dealer. It's how she can walk into the gallery, immediately commanding the man's interest. "Hey, I'll call you back." She pretends to care about the showing, pausing to inspect a piece of art, which can only be described as an abstraction or deconstruction of a self-portrait, while the man joins her to admire the art. She doesn't need to say anything. It's seamless. He offers her a job after she willingly interprets the portrait, calling it a "resounding portrayal of how there is only one person that can see the person beneath the persona, and that's you, your own self... this piece causes viewers to inspect the severity of being unable to see themselves. If you can't, how can anyone?"

He admires the interpretation, doing his best to flatter her as much as he explains the origins of both the piece and the current show. "We've had some struggles getting the gallery back on good footing since the departure of our last owner." The gallery switched owners, the man's unwillingness to speak about it is all Olivia needs to understand that there was a falling out. Probably about money (when is it not?). There was a betrayal, and now it's down to the few employees that are left, scrambling to understand how to run a business they've only just begun to learn about. He turns to her and asks her, "Where's your gallery?"

A perfect opportunity for her to conjure up a story. Yet it's actually quite surprising to see how she doesn't waste the breath. No fabrications or lies, no fictional backstory: She says she'll be the new dealer. He takes it in stride, "Oh my god, really?"

Olivia finds her financial footing.

"Let me show you what else we've got," her employee says. He escorts her into the back, a few rooms full of unsold sculptures and paintings. "I'm so sad about this one," he says, holding up a canvas. "Not a single one sold. It's why Clara bailed. I don't really blame her... but she could have least been good about it."

But everything's fine now because Olivia is here.

"Your office!" He grabs her lightly by the hand, a gesture that might have caught her off guard, resulting in panic, days ago, but in the moment, cast against all that pain, the virus firing all senses and cells on all cylinders, she thinks nothing of it. A vote for false kindness.

At the end of this transaction is an office, hers, and the thought that he won't lose his job, and who knows, there could be a promotion at the end of it.

He talks about Clara, but Olivia shakes her head. "I don't care."

"Right," he bows. "I'm sorry. I shouldn't carry this."

A vein in her neck bulges; her mouth suddenly dry, throat scratchy, she makes it clear that he must leave her. Now.

"Sorry," he says.

She slams the door on him.

No one will see her this way.

The next attack is far worse, vastly different, than the last. She can't stop coughing, and her employee (she doesn't care to know anyone's name when few ever bothered to learn hers) starts knocking, "Are you okay?" Ignore. Every bit of energy goes to fighting back an intense pain originating from the seat of her brain, radiating out like electricity through both arms and legs. She focuses on her breath, doing all she can to endure the attack.

After yet another fit of coughing, she senses something's off. Catching her reflection against one of the chrome frames installed in the office, she sees it, half of her face has sunk, gone lifeless, her nerves bankrupt.

Mortified, she lets out a scream.

"Oh my god! I don't know what's happening! I'm calling 911!"

"No!" she shouts, voice cracking.

"Then what do you want me to do?"

Olivia can't ever know why it happens, only that she bothers to say it: "Open the door! Film everything!" The employee turns the knob, finds that it's mysteriously now unlocked. She flails around on the ground, the pain giving her pleasure. The pleasure… it'll be interpreted later as a demonstration of how ecstasy can be thought of across a spectrum.

Even before he takes out his phone and starts recording, there's the idea that someone else is watching. The employee looks around the room, confused.

She screams, pulling him back into the moment.

The spit, the blood, the horrific look upon her face, it is so overwhelming, it comes off as a spectacle. And after the peak of the attack relents, Olivia plays out the rest of it like she had meant for this to be the case all along. As a new wave of euphoria cradles her, so too does she cradle the opportunity of becoming the next viral demonstration.

The video is saved and eventually uploaded, only a tease, online. It has everything to do with her intent that makes it go viral. When people figure out who she is, and where she works, calling her an art dealer and performance artist, Olivia only needs to continue to stoke the flame of art world obsession.

Looking back at how it plays out, the media and its connoisseurs treat the video and subsequent performance like a virus. It takes hold quickly, in the same afternoon; by the dawn of the third day, Olivia has offers from managers and international dealers seeking to book her for in-person performances.

The art world desires to witness the performance live. She says yes.

After another attack happens in private where she is keen enough to hit record on a camera, centralized in her studio apartment, she records and streams it live. The world watches as her eyes drip red with blood, her body succumbing to an alarming episode of successive seizures, every vein in her body bulging to reveal a web. People watch. People wonder. After it's over and she looks gorgeous for the camera, exactly her intention, people get to talking.

She leaves the art gallery, having no use for it. Never worked a day there, yet because it became the setting for her first performance, it receives a steady stream of people visiting, buying art, just so that they can say that they own something she may have held.

A sold out tour, like something expected of a Grammy winning pop star. Olivia builds up an entourage of people that she never speaks to; they make sure she has what she wants, is protected from the public eye, and they work on ensuring that her persona, the artist commodified, is worked through without wasted opportunities.

After a particularly difficult attack in Mexico City, where Olivia goes over the 35-minute runtime of her performance, causing many in the audience to leave, fearing how her body can levitate, can lose its hair and teeth, the virus taking its share of her energy so that Olivia may continue to use it, it becomes a turning point. The next show is cancelled, not because people remember what happened but rather because Olivia worries about what the next attack will bring.

It would be more accurate to say that the virus takes her on tour, not the other way around.

She'll see it on the news—a man sets himself on fire—and won't think anything of it. When she's checking her email late one night, a newsletter from a prominent publication rounding up their viral stories for the week lands in her inbox, she makes a point to skim it at least, because this is what she's trying to do. Be a person in a society that sees people as people connected and keenly aware of every cultural element of the discourse.

Second from the top, a story about self-immolation. In the story, there's mention of that man from the news, yet the journalist finds more interest in how "with so many in attendance, people did so little to stop him." There's a picture of three people around the charred body. Alarming stuff. Yet for Olivia, it barely registers.

There's going to be another attack.

It'll save her until it doesn't. The latter is what begins to be her final fear. One night, on a private jet headed to Paris, second to the last stop on her tour, she remembers him. To her surprise, she tries to remember details, but it's all gone, every memory.

Will? Is that his name? Yes, it resurfaces in a half-remembered dream, the grief share group, the way it made her feel horrible. She finds his number, and texts him the question he never answered: "What do you have?"

CHAPTER
XVII

Will suffers another attack shortly after waking up on what should be a momentous occasion. Today is the day—he heads up the entire department, a new promotion—and now he's late. He wakes up to heart palpitations, by the time he gets out of bed, he's getting hit by noxious waves of pain. It makes it difficult to breathe, every single breath surging pure fire. He calls out a name, "Roderick." It's a name unfamiliar, a stranger that had been with him all this time. Since first bite.

"Fuck," he winces, barely making it to the kitchen.

What's he looking for? Opening and closing drawers, it's evident that he's searching for a consolation. If he doesn't want to feel this, how about feeling something else?

The height of another tremor, Will reaches for a fork and begins digging into the soft flesh of his palm. Anything, feel anything. The name hangs there. Roderick.

Could it be? This is it? The virus shows itself and he doesn't like what it feels like, the crash. The fork's teeth dig in and tear at the flesh, red-purple distension at the site of the self-harm. Will winces, it's simply not enough.

Fork tossed aside, Will reaches for one of the knives. It's like so long ago, the cut across a palm. What was his name again? There's too much on his mind to think about Zaff. It's all lost to the anguish. Roderick was healthy once, look what happened to him.

Will wastes an hour fighting off the waves. The worst of it happens when he's busy cutting his left arm and he slips, digging a little too deep, leaving him with two problems: the attack and potentially bleeding out.

He wraps a shirt around the wound, the blood collecting in its fibers, turning it from a light blue to a dark red, borderline black.

Must be thinking, Why won't this end? The previous attacks never lasted any longer than a few minutes. It's taking most of his morning.

Remembering the importance of the morning, Will climbs to his feet, determined to fight through the attack, preempting the euphoria, because today is his day. He has wanted this since he walked into Kelso's office. It has everything to do with being the person everyone expects him to be. So what if he bleeds onto the carpet? Every drop will be replaced.

The water pooling at his feet changes color, Will unwrapping the makeshift bandage. He can feel the electricity surging through his brain.

"No, not now," he blinks, seeing dark spots. It could be a seizure. The last one took him out for two hours, half of it battling the actual seizure and the other hour given to absolute mental and physical exhaustion.

He refuses to give in, grabbing the shampoo, fighting through the pain, now his left arm refuses to cooperate, while he lathers the substance in his hair. He feels the hair knot against his hand, another counterattack, Roderick offering the first of many cosmetic blemishes.

When he retracts his hand, he takes a knot of his own hair.

Vanity plays its part, surely. The seizure ongoing causes less concern: It's the fact that he's shedding his hair that gets Will succumbing to the realities of the virus's destructive path.

His vision sparkling and going dim, he has just enough in him to run the warm water over his head, seeing his short hair pulled and carried with the current. When he shuts off the faucet, the floor of the tub is a mess of dark black hair. Running a hand over his head, he expects to feel something, instead his touch grazing against a newly bald dome.

"No," he shudders.

The seizure runs its course, he can reach a mirror, vision offering a glimpse at his new look. His eyelids are puffy, hair missing, skin dangerously pale, and he's still bleeding.

The thought occurs to call someone; it's evident in how he retrieves his phone from the bedroom, every footstep causing a heavy blow, damage dealt to an already labored body.

Scrolling through numbers, it's like he can't concentrate.

The mind starts to drift at some point. It could be that he's thinking this is all a nightmare, not at all real. If only he could hide in the illusion for a while. Instead, his phone lights up. Someone calling him.

He swallows, picking up.

"Hello?"

He isn't the one saying hello.

"Will? Are you there?"

A familiar voice. Amber, the receptionist. He might have flirted with her once, maybe gone on a date. Make that two. His mind is sludge, tongue caught between his molars.

"It's me, Amber. Babe, are you okay? It's like 10:30AM. The big meeting is in 15 minutes. They were expecting you by now."

This is the part where he's probably thinking about the comedown, the euphoria after the attack lapses. He'll keep fighting and sure he might be late, but he'll be able to persuade everyone. Will has enjoyed a nice run of manipulation and making the best of a defunct situation, he has ideas that'll involve explaining everything and still getting ahead.

There's something weakening his plans, though. Roderick has a very particular and demanding trajectory, one that holds onto a few surprises. For one thing, Will doesn't want to admit that there will be an attack that never ends. He hasn't been as observant during the past couple weeks. Too preoccupied with being at the helm of everyone's attention. It's to be expected. The euphoria is called that for a reason; it conceals the inevitable depression, the pull to yet another relapse of pain, anguish, and doubt. He became all things to all these people, a veritable charismatic individual. Life of the party. Yet, a person needs life if there's anything to fuel a party. He needs to understand that they only ever bought in because he had the helm of all power. Roderick glows like the source of some untold power, when really it wants the same thing everyone wants, to flourish. It does not want to suffer.

Could be that Roderick knows that his body and mind is nearing its limit. Everything ends, nothing is forever; Will could be reaching the breaking point.

Roderick knows.

And by that one could say, Zaff saw it coming from the first time he walked into his life.

"Will!" It isn't the first time she's called out his name. He'd reply if he could. Instead, his mind has slipped into a deep sleep. Fail safe, damage repair mode for a mind when it can do very little to fend off the current onslaught.

When he wakes back up, he can't move. He has no understanding of where he is, only that he is awake and what's clear and present is the pain. It's a constant, deep pain surging from his stomach. It feels like there could be something in there, wanting out.

Will tries to move. He can't. His body remains partly in the doorway leading to his bedroom and on the floor of the lone hallway of the apartment. The body is on its left side, the dead weight of an immobile body restricting blood flow. He can feel the tingly sensation of his nerves cut off and struggling. The arm will fail to work, that is, if he could even move it. This will undoubtedly remain as-is, the situation identical as he discovers that perhaps the seizure wasn't over after all. He could have hit his head on the way down. After the fall, he could have lost consciousness. Where's his phone? It's just out of reach, temporarily forgotten.

He can breathe, the rise and fall of his chest is proof, but slowly things start to lose their luster. Among them, Will simply cannot get past the fact that he cannot move. It's no longer about symptoms; he's starting to believe that this could be it.

Without any ability to move one's body, thoughts are all you have. One must imagine what Will is thinking about. What is he going through?

The superficial side of things, he thinks about his career. He went from fraud to a featured employee, new promotion helping him climb to second in command. Cybersecurity expert. The best in the business. Everyone wants a piece of him, or rather everyone wants to be in the Will business. They know him by name, and he's invited to every party in the city. Somehow his name has reached the fashion industry. They put him on all the runway shows, fashion week happening recently, he was invited to all of the best events. A few by request, though he chose the largest power move of all—no-showing every event. It only made people more curious about him. Who is this guy, this Will? He came out of nowhere, and has an entire industry reexamining their security protocols.

He has the entire industry in the palm of his hands. Invigorating given a short time ago he was a vagrant slushing around with no opportunities.

It's safe to assume he thinks very highly of himself.

On a deeper level, there are concerns dealing with his identity. Who is he, now? Is it any different from the person he used to be a short while ago? The very same person that chased the crash, willingly subjecting his own body and mind to pathogens... what changed and what remains? Will does not look to be the same person. He has certainly let his ego get the better of his clarity. In all the noise, he felt alive. Certainly, his actions and behavior reflect his priorities. Amber is only of value to him because she is attractive, good arm candy. How fickle indeed.

Though this is conjecture, it's fairly evident that Will has walked the same paths, donned the same archetypal suits and style of dress; he has become executive according to the term.

Why would he have done any different, seeing how his goals were always to be at the seat of some degree of power? Never mind the curse. What Zaff had called a curse, Will saw as an opportunity. At its essence, an opportunity is a transactional exchange, something inflicted upon any and all parties involved. The curse Will carried, it had no other priority in mind except to see to it that Will could climb the ladder, making sure to step on some toes and shatter some egos along the way.

That is confirmed when there's a call from Kelso, three actually. They go to voicemail. He leaves a voicemail. Three. Minutes later, enough time for word to proliferate across the company, the gossip blossoms and Will's phone blows up.

Everyone wants a piece of his power.

The curse, it can certainly backfire.

Will sees none of this. He floats in the ethers of his mind, consumed by the pain and how it so seamlessly calls upon a person's innermost demons.

In Will's case, he endures a vision of losing his job, the same scam and public humiliation he had incurred years ago, after he was discovered to be an extortionist.

The phone battery starts to drain, a ceaseless outpour of notifications.

Will lets out a cough. A breakthrough in regaining control of his body.

Perhaps that's enough struggle. Roderick relents, freeing his arms. The left is unresponsive, potential nerve damage, but he still has use of his right. Will rolls onto his shoulder, tipping his body over so that he is able to lay straight on his back.

Relieved, he coughs. Does so a second time.

The coughing is forced, entirely artificial. At first, his coughs could be interpreted as a call for help. Unable to speak, he makes a noise, the coughing aimed to draw attention. He must have figured there would be someone around that would help him. And so eventually the coughing takes on a different purpose. His coughs are battle cries, the continued use of his lungs gives way to his ability to turn his neck, move his fingers; his body comes back to life.

Though he tries to speak, Will can only manage a hiss of hot air.

Without words, he has only body language. He's able to throw his fist against the wall, and then drive it into the hardwood floor. He's trying to get someone's attention. By now he must sense that people are nearby. He can hear them walking from their vehicles to their respective apartments. Someone should be able to hear him, right?

His 10:30AM meeting is over. Long gone.

The workday is over. People have other things in mind.

Will takes a look around at what is within an arm's reach. The phone glows, he reaches for it. His fingers are clumsy, slow, responding with a delay. They lock at the joints, causing him to wince. At least the waves of pain seem to have slowed. A few more reaches, his index and middle fingers wedging the side of the phone, he gains access.

Left arm remains lifeless. Will uses the area between chest and chin to prop the phone. The screen lights up and reveals hundreds of missed notifications. He knows something happened. A quick skim as he stumbles to unlock his passcode using his one hand, he sees text previews like "where are you" and "did you seriously ghost them are you crazy!" This is the sort of thing that you see as a trickle of a potential career-ender, a fiasco where an industry gets talking, and a person is often put in the position of being outed as inferior and inadequate.

They all want something.

Will is vulnerable and no longer able to utilize the euphoric effects of the virus, he is a name and a number being led to the slaughter.

He texts Amber, "I need help."

There's no immediate reply.

Unsure of how much time he has before the attack worsens, he switches on the emergency signal, the call going out to everyone in his contacts list. There's only one reply, "Why did you quit your job today?" Will coughs, his throat raw from overuse, he struggles to input a reply.

"I didn't quit" and then "I need help."

No reply.

Will taps another notification, sending him straight into the depths of social media. It's an article about him. Published approximately an hour ago, the article discusses the supposed "walkout" of "a new executive…" which in and of itself is not great given the disrespect at such a high level; yet what makes it worse is that the article dredges up his past. It reserves three paragraphs for his past, the very same past that he had hoped to learn and walk away from. However, it doesn't appear like Will has learned a whole lot, does it?

The article has gone viral. Viruses like people outnumber us. The abundance of their pull can put a scare on anyone's face. Will might be scared, there isn't a whole lot of a reaction as he reads, scrolling through the various threads online tearing him apart. He's a fraud. He has always been a fraud. This walkout, this complete abandonment during a pivotal meeting, is used as declaration of his true motives. Is the silver lining still visible?

Does he still think he'll be able to roll this all back post-attack?

The attack, it seems to react to such a thought.

He winces, phone sliding off his chest. It starts deep in his stomach. Another wave, yet this one holds on. It doesn't dissipate.

The ache is constant, yet dull enough that he seems to feel around for the source. His fingers push into the soft area of his stomach. Push until he feels it push back. Will coughs, can't stop coughing. There's no running away from what endures in his stomach. Like the rash, he can feel it moving, churning his stomach acids. There should be nausea, but instead he can't stop coughing. His stomach begins to grow, bloating until it's the size of a basketball.

The growth happens in slow motion. It would be called a marvelous sight, even a miracle, in other circumstances. For Will, it is an impossibility, one that makes him think about what might be causing the growth.

Trying again, he pushes against the bloat.

He feels his stomach lining reverberate, launching an equal and requisite response; the sensation must be strange, how else could one describe it? The response is visible on the surface, his abdominal muscles clenching and then releasing. Will dares another attempt, yet it's perhaps one too many because his press results in an intense pressure. The attack holds onto that pressure, it's palpable enough that he claws at his throat and stomach, his fingernails catching skin, leaving red trails. When he goes for his stomach a second time, his index finger catches, the nail peeling back effortlessly. The powerful sting is slow to register, but when it does, Will lets out the first audible sound since Roderick pulled him down for the final attack.

"Help!"

There'll be nobody to help.

He turns this way, looking at us. There'll be no reaction.

All we do is what we've done all along.

We watch.

He never gets to the office. The attack won't let go. This could be it.

It might be the final and most fatal attack. Roderick making it clear, the curse is never one-sided. It always demands double.

It would have been a lie to say that it was clear, the onset of the final attack obvious. It never works that way. The virus incubates and symptoms show often too late. By then it has already set foot inside one's cellular structure; the virus has made its host a place of worship and subsequent sacrilege. Will's body will continue to bloat. It doesn't explode; the entirely of the virus remains safe in his skin.

A text message. He doesn't recognize the name, not at first. A half-memory snaps to, remembering a different time. When he chased, he wasn't alone. She was there, with him.

Why can't he remember?

"What do you have?"

The text message is a question. Barely able to reach the phone, he labors over a reply.

His final text, will be his final words.

"I don't know."

CHAPTER

XVIII

The final stop on the tour. Olivia isn't feeling well and, much to her surprise, she doesn't want another attack. Not right now. Enough with the crashing, she just wants to feel the light. It's not that simple though. Her fans want to see her fall apart. She finds it all so ironic that the moment she has people's validation, she no longer wants to feel that way. The symptoms never being the same has a lot to do with it. Her stop in Berlin was a disappointment. The attack was just her throwing up for 45 minutes. People reviewed the performance poorly and now she refuses to look at social media. The hate and vitriol is enough to ruin her mental health.

Nobody cares.

They just want to see her squirm. See her pain, experience pleasure when they see a person doing worse than them. She's a trainwreck, that's how she's marketed worldwide. Go see the trainwreck, she literally shits herself and goes crazy on stage.

Is this about art?

Probably not, if you asked people. The art dealers have something on the line. They make money off her misery. Officially, she's an artist, when really, she's dying for everyone. Validation will do that to a person. It'll make you wish you were dead.

Sweden is fanatical about her videos and her "art." Olivia walks off the plane and there's a crowd already gathered. She can't really concentrate, all the compliments hit her flatly.

Thank you.

You're so kind.

Of course, I'll sign it.

Olivia goes through the motions and her entourage can clearly see that she's suffering. They push the people aside, clearing a path, and they get to the vehicle waiting for her at arrival, an escape and straight shot to her hotel room. She finds out it's a 5 star hotel and they booked the penthouse. You only get treated this way when there's something on the line.

Her "health" is constantly under watch.

There's one member of the entourage whose job is to check her temperature every 15 minutes. Olivia is starting to nod off when this person once again opens her mouth, slipping a thermometer between her lips.

"Oh," Olivia jolts awake.

The person isn't even gentle about it.

"Under your tongue," she says.

Olivia complies.

Is this the life people want, full of fake friendships and distance? Olivia must have expected the less than rosy and cheery veneer. The luster of celebrity is seeing it from the outside; when you're in it, there's simply more stress and anxiety. A person no longer is a person and can never fully live in their bodies because they are commodified. People will feel entitled to a celebrity, and there's always something happening, people trying to take her down.

What's the latest?

A quick look online and it seems people are talking about how she's a fake. She isn't actually sick, and all these crazy symptoms don't add up. They are right about that: They don't add up. They aren't supposed to. There's something novel and new to her affliction.

The affinites of the world and the armchair casuals unite. There's something different about this one.

There's a whole thread about how she uses special effects.

Another thread talks about her dating life, when she actually hasn't been with anyone since Will. No interest, even less so now that she can't be sure if there's anyone to trust. They match her with anyone that's been photographed with her more than once. They want her to be connected, celebrities given personal demands.

This is why she is so private about everything. Never alone, she has her entourage.

The thermometer beeps, she looks at the temperature, seems adequate. A fever at all times. If she wasn't symptomatic, they would be worried.

In the penthouse, they never leave her side. By now everyone in the entourage has seen every side of her, every single mood.

"I wish I could be alone," she says.

Nobody cares.

They watch TV and tend to their own devices. Olivia is a caged commodity. She lies down on the bed and dozes off.

The attack hits her while she's unconscious. She wakes up to one member of her entourage injecting something into her vein. They don't bother telling her what it is but she knows. Morphine. Really though, the attack has been ongoing for almost a day now. They don't see it but they also don't care.

We wait. We'd tell her it won't be long now. But she doesn't need to know. You're never alone when someone wants something.

Once again under the veil of a deep drugged up sleep, Olivia is assessed, the picture being painted is her upcoming death. No doubt about it, we expect the same kind of attraction that drew her to the virus in the first place. Olivia will have one last performance and it'll be the one that ends with her dying in front of the camera. A public suicide?

Close. It'll be up to interpretation. Every fan is entitled to their own aches and pains.

While she's out cold, the entourage draws blood. They take her temperature and tend to her body. In the interest of time, they get started on grooming. Sponge bath, shaving her legs, making sure her body is primed for the last performance of the tour.

She wakes up between doses.

"What are you doing?"

They ignore her questions, pumping her with another drug. It'll help allay the symptoms, and furthermore, they'll ensure that they have her under the influence to better serve the performance. The fact that each stop since Berlin has resulted in a more "profound" (read: debilitating) performances than the last is no accident. They were hired to ensure that she is at her best at every stop. If her health suffers...

Well that's kind of the point.

An hour before she needs to be at the venue, they remove an IV drip and tell her that "she needs to eat something."

"I'm not hungry," she groans, not quite sure where she is.

"You'll need to, or else you won't have anything to show."

They're talking about vomit. An empty stomach leaves less to be desired. They'll force feed her if they have to. Room service is ordered and soon they have chicken fingers, a burger, and fries filed into the room. It's on her rider. Somewhere they mentioned that she loves simple foods, nothing quite like a burger. It's not entirely true, and again it doesn't matter. She is force fed bites of the burger.

Olivia gags.

"Swallow." They say. "Swallow!"

After she finishes the burger, they check her temperature, her heartbeat. Another dose is administered. They help her put on a dress, and then it's time to go to the venue.

A limousine is waiting for them out front. The glamour is surely there, the impression that she is being treated to the light. Really though, she couldn't tell anyone if she's currently suffering or if she's euphoric. It's all the same.

On the ride to the venue, they brief her on the details.

"The box office tells us there'll be 1,800 capacity. Sold out. This is a big one. Last of the tour. You realize how important that is, right?"

She nods.

"Good. Tonight's the night to do something new. Leave them hanging."

There's another voice: "We were actually wondering if… you might be willing to try dismemberment?"

She doesn't quite understand.

"Just a finger. It doesn't need to be a lot."

A member of the entourage hands her a pair of scissors.

"Use it. They use it to cut meat and bone. It's sharp."

"Yeah, management really likes the idea of your body changing with every tour. People change as the years go by. Musicians get tattoos. We're thinking… scars, missing limbs."

Someone else suggests that "you don't need both eyes, you know."

She takes it all in. They don't give her a choice.

Looking down at the scissors, she can almost see her face reflected back. Sunken eyes; she doesn't remember dressing like a doll. They've made her out to be a motif.

When they get to the venue, they pull around back, entourage filing out first, creating a protective barrier.

"Out. Come on. Out!" She is escorted out, directed into the venue, told not to look at anyone. "No eye contact." The halls are lined with people interested in a piece of her. She is led to yet another private room where only her aide remains.

Checking her temperature, giving her another dose.

Someone knocks on the door and tells her she's got 10 minutes.

"Ready?"

Olivia has no choice. She has done this before. An attack on command, she stands up, looks at herself in the mirror, and gives in to the fact that she doesn't recognize herself. Maybe it's for the better. It's unclear whether Olivia would have wanted things to be this way.

The stage is bare save for a mic stand and a stool. It could be a standup comedy routine, nobody would be able to tell the difference. The place is packed. Some people stand in the aisles, ignoring fire safety precautions. The stagehand gives her the signal. The lights go up and there's music. A large backlit screen plays back the viral videos and other footage of her at the height of an attack. This is torture, a vivid depiction of a person in pain. There's applause, a chant forming, her name, "Oh-livy-ah, oh-livy-ah, oh-livy-ah," It gains strength and quickly takes the room.

It's like this at every stop. She waits until the chant starts to turn, becoming hostile, and then walks out. Olivia doesn't acknowledge the crowd. She takes the microphone and starts talking about how "she doesn't feel well" and that she "hasn't felt well for a while." The wording changes sometimes but it's the same as always, "I think there's something going around."

People cheer at the mention of her health.

A cough. There's some applause.

She spits some phlegm, the room falling silent.

It's time. She's going to do it! The anticipation is palpable, yet Olivia takes her time. She starts coughing again and soon she cannot stop. Her face reddens, veins in her throat visible to onlookers. A preamble of sorts, Olivia has learned how to stress her body. These aren't real symptoms, anyone that has seen her behind the scenes knows that. But it is indeed a performance, and people have paid to see her pain. Self-inflicted, it does come off odd. A few boos extend from the audience. From the side of the stage, a member of her entourage frowns, gives her a cue to ratchet things up.

Go for it.

She remembers the pair of scissors.

No, she doesn't have a choice.

The attack does not arrive because she's had it all along. Her skin glistens with sweat, the pressure is immense. Her coughing evolves to dry heaves. She reveals the scissors, mumbling into the microphone, "It won't stop. Why won't it stop?!"

She stabs herself with the pair of scissors twice in the chest.

A few gasps from the crowd.

Olivia's dress is soaked in no time so she pulls it off, the blood becoming like a second outfit, concealing her naked body. She slashes at her stomach, taking the pair of scissors and announcing to the audience that "she doesn't want to live this way" and does what was prompted on the ride to the venue. She loses her left pinky and tosses it into the crowd. Nobody wants it, people move out of the way, keeping their distance. It seems she is spoiled goods. They like a show, not part of her. The stage gets sticky, the amount of blood loss from repeated stabbings becomes suspect. At some point she is going to pass out, right?

It's a riveting performance. Different, but good. Not great, a B+ currently and Olivia is given another cue proving that she isn't meeting the mark.

Fine, if that's what they want, she'll do it.

Olivia sticks out her tongue, the scissors placed at the base of the organ. You can see people looking away, shutting their eyes. She's going to do it. She's really going to do it.

As she clamps down, she projectile vomits into the audience. The first couple rows get hit with a brownish-red concoction of partially digested food and something else. She keeps throwing up, really she can't stop. A little late but better than never, she experiences excruciating stomach pain to match with the repeated upchucks. The crowd starts to leave, the room smelling horrible. Some stick around, though it must be noted, here and now, that some pathogens can be contracted by airborne droplets. What was the number of people in attendance again, 1800?

A solid super spreader.

It could be that Olivia saw it as an opportunity. Spread her misery. Anyway, that's what people want to see. Other people doing poorly.

She slips and falls offstage. At some point it all starts coming out, urine down her leg, the horrible blotch of excrement smeared into an unrecognizable mess. The venue clears out the majority of the audience.

To make sure, she goes back to her tongue, says something like "by popular demand," and she slices through it like butter. Her mouth swells and overflows with blood. The tongue is raised, a photographer at stage right takes a photo. A dozen are left, mostly in the balcony seats. The entourage doesn't know what to do. One member leaves, perhaps understanding that this is it, the line has been crossed. You can't save Olivia, she's done. Fully broken.

Where's the light?

She can't find it, so she goes searching, the scissors used to open up her stomach. The fact that she can do so much damage without losing consciousness is a marvel all its own. This is the part where we start paying attention because she should have been dead by now.

Instead, she holds onto her entrails, a clumsy smile, and then she spits out more blood. Everyone that stuck around files out of the venue. They leave Olivia to die alone.

What they don't see is how she does what Zaff did. She presses down on every wound and undoes the damage. The attack and the euphoria are identical; she's so drugged up she can't tell the difference. In her dying moments, she glimpsed how it would look to end this way. Perhaps she notices, or rather realizes that she might have desired something more of her life… it's unclear. What is clear is that she has at least one more attack.

She says his name, her tongue returned, "Zaff."

It is Zaff. It could go by any name, but it's the one that comes to mind. She doesn't remember him, only the bite. She remembers his own attacks, and she remembers the first time she felt the symptoms.

How simple it used to be, the day in the gallery, the moment of viral sensation. Olivia returns to form, the deadly self-massacre existing only in their minds, the audience and the world believing her to be dead, yet there is no trace of her mutilation.

Sniff the air, there's not even an odor.

Olivia leaves the stage and navigates her way through the venue. Everyone cleared out, perhaps fearing the worst. Legal action, the cops, who really knows. What is known is that they fled the scene. They were witness to a public suicide.

We could but instead we wait.

With nowhere else to go and the worry that the next attack could be it, she uses her last moment of lightness to leave the country. She is her own entourage, retracing her steps, eating expensive meals, watching tons of movies. If anyone asks, she isn't Olivia. She gives them different names and then quickly changes the subject.

"Do you know Zaff?"

She isn't looking. He's right there, attacking her immune system.

When she finally lands stateside, she remembers him. He texted her back.

"I don't know." But she does. She enjoys the drive back through familiar streets, the same apartment building. The door is unlocked. She sees what we saw. His body is still fresh, death was only minutes ago. Olivia kneels down next to the body.

She thinks of all the people in attendance that night.

Zaff. The name climbs to the surface of her consciousness. Lying next to him, she notices how his body is still warm. For a time, she lays there, unwilling to accept what is about to arrive. When the attack happens, she walks into the bedroom, falls into the bed, and gives in. By giving in, her body doesn't fight. A silent cry, her tears dampen the sheets, eventually turning red. Her body hemorrhages, and as she loses her grip on reality, it's the vomit in her mouth that chokes her to death. The last sounds of her choking, the body finally giving out. It plays itself out somberly. Truly, a sad sight, two beings that might have understood how much they meant to each other, if they could see past all the ache and hurt that had denied them their ability to see life for what it was. Here, in this apartment, they are two bodies that will go unnoticed by others. Similar to their lives, in death they are invisible. Used, they were abused for the sake of other people's opportunities. What are civil rights when a person can be so cruel to another? In death, they are identical. They are useless, bodies ready for burial. Who gets to say what becomes of the body? Cremation, burial? What about the headstone? And what happens to their legacy, if they have one? Perhaps the answer to all of the above is for us to decide. We've waited and watched for so long, understanding that there would be something to blossom from all their misery.

The answer is a harvest.

We've done this all before.

THE
SOURCE

You can't wait until the body goes cold. We get to work in a timely manner. Roderick's body was unusable but both Will and Olivia's bodies are primed for the harvest. When it's clear that there will be no more surprises, we put in the call. Those on #bodyharvest know what to do. We only need five to fully deal with the bodies. There are six of us by the time we've conditioned the apartment in plastic. Last one there acts as lookout.

I don't make the rules. He does. Kaz puts in the plea.

A bargain of sorts, everyone that harvests is trusted to collect. Being this close to the bodies, we can surely contract it too. If that's what you want. I can't speak for everyone but I have been watching since they got to chasing. I've been here longer than most. It makes sense that I have a part in this too. Kaz selected me precisely because I'm committed. Months of watching and following. Seeing it all.

That's commitment. Bert is here, which is cool.

He makes the first cut, both bodies moved from their death beds and brought into the living room. Amid all the plastic, we have coolers ready. No part of the body goes to waste. Fire up the bone saws, the apartment coming to life with activity.

First, the arms then the legs. The last to be dealt with is the head.

But we don't waste any time. I make sure to file everything away, each part an opportunity and a sale. There are affinites out there that'll pay anything. They'll do anything. I mean just look at us.

We always get the source.

Times like these, we are brutally organized because we take pride in being there first. The excitement gets to me; I almost drop one of Olivia's organs.

Careful.

We have to be careful. Though we are organized, we are not above failure. It could happen. I recall an attempt on the #bodyharvest subcategory, following someone terminal until they were dead. The problem was that the neighbors got involved. It became a whole thing. Those affinites are still doing jail time.

No worries though.

We'll be fine. I made sure of it.

The blood is collected, though it does start to coagulate and become unwieldy, we have enough vials to get an offering. I get a text from Kaz, asking for a progress report.

I give him the best kind of update.

Almost done here.

It's tough not to think about them, knowing them so well. I'm probably the closest to being someone that could tell their story. No one will care though, not about two "losers" like them. Nobody cares unless there's something to take. We're taking it all.

I do think about it. About them.

Maybe a little paragraph somewhere. To think so many people are invisible their entire lives and they just as easily are taken, left without a trace. All that life and nothing to show for it. They won't even be patient zeroes. Roderick was clever. He saw us watching. He knew that he was dying and what better way than to make it so that there's nothing for us to take.

The signs are always there. We are human, after all, capable of making mistakes. We made one with him, but we didn't with Will and Olivia. They were perfect, really they were.

I think that's what I'd say. Maybe I'll share it with the Source, telling them about what Will did during the brink of the virus, how Olivia became an acclaimed performance artist. Give them the high and they'll undoubtedly seek out the next low.

It's interesting, you know, our relationship with pathogens. We see them as parasites, as things that take, when really they are alive, struggling to exist, just like us. Though they are invisible to the human eye, we feel them more deeply, perhaps the deepest of which being how we must endure their worst before we can learn and grow. They change our lives, every single time. It could be a passing cold or an ongoing spell, the virus grips hold of our lives. It makes itself known, perhaps because it was not given the same body, the same extent we have been given. It needs help and we unknowingly give it life. They are so damn resilient, eventually no antibiotic or vaccine will combat them. Give a virus time and it'll grow to change the world.

Affinites or not, we see a new world too. It's just too bad about the other body. I made sure to see to it that neither Will nor Olivia will have anyone looking for them. That's kind of how this works. The hosts end up isolated, unknowingly disconnected from a network of people.

But yeah, I'll write about them.

No telling when, or if anyone will read it, but I'll write it out.

Kaz asking for another update.

We're done. The bodies are filed away in a succession of coolers. They see about transporting them safely and unsuspectingly while me and another affinite deal with the clutter. We could set fire to the spot, but no. That's excessive. Instead, we bleach the surfaces, the apartment smelling powerfully of a hospital by the time we're done with it. The landlord will find the spot in a few days, maybe a week. He'll have no problem renting the place out.

That's not what this is really about. It's not about them, Will and

Olivia, how they simply vanish. Their disappearance should cause a scene, people looking for them. But it won't.

They are simply not there.

"It's okay. Don't worry. Your misery has been useful."

My parting words.

One last look at the apartment, I'm the last to leave. No time for feeling somber or sad about it, we have a lot of work to do. I think I'll stick to the heart, Olivia's. That's what I tell Kaz. He gives me a thumbs up. I find the cooler and go about my way. Everyone disperses the same way they arrived, individual cars, each with a few coolers. They'll drop off and then wait it out. It won't be long until the boards are talking about it.

We were there first, the Source.

Not today but maybe tomorrow or the next day, it will circulate. The virus will make its introduction. A patient zero will be named and their name will be mine.

MICHAEL J. SEIDLINGER

MICHAEL J. SEIDLINGER is the Filipino-American author of *The Body Harvest*, *Anybody Home?*, *Tekken 5* (Boss Fight Books), and other books. He has written for, among others, *Wired*, *Buzzfeed*, *Polygon*, *The Believer*, and *Publishers Weekly*. He teaches at Portland State University and has led workshops at Catapult, Kettle Pond Writer's Conference, and Sarah Lawrence. He is represented by Lane Heymont at The Tobias Literary Agency. You can find him at michaeljseidlinger.com.

ANYBODY HOME?
Michael J. Seidlinger

HEXIS
Charlene Elsby

CHARCOAL
Garrett Cook

THE LONGEST SUMMER
Alexandrine Ogundimu

PEST
Michael Cisco

LES FEMMES GROTESQUES
Victoria Dalpe

THE PAIN EATER
Kyle Muntz

THE ECSTASY OF AGONY
Wrath James White

EVERYTHING THE DARRKNESS EATS
Eric LaRocca

THE BLACK TREE ATOP THE HILL
Karla Yvette

I DIED TOO, BUT THEY HAVEN'T BURIED ME YET
Ross Jeffery

WE PUT THE LIT IN LITERARY
clashbooks.com

 @clashbooks @clashbooks /clashbooks

Email
clashmediabooks@gmail.com

9 781955 904872